Blue Taxis

Blue Taxis

Stories About Africa
by Eileen Drew

Foreword by Rosellen Brown
Designed and Illustrated
by R. W. Scholes

MILKWEED EDITIONS

BLUE TAXIS

Printed in the United States of America
Published in 1989 by *Milkweed Editions*
Post Office Box 3226
Minneapolis, Minnesota 55403
Books may be ordered from the above address
92 91 90 89   4 3 2 1

ISBN 0-915943-41-7

Publication of *Blue Taxis*, the second Milkweed National Fiction Prize winner, is made possible by grant support from the Dayton Hudson Foundation for Dayton's and Target Stores, and by support from the Jerome Foundation, the Arts Development Fund of United Arts, the Literature Program of the National Endowment for the Arts, the Minnesota State Arts Board with funds appropriated by the State legislature, and with additional funding from the McKnight Foundation, and by the support of generous individuals.

The author wishes to acknowledge the publication of several of the stories in this collection in the following publication:

"Ancient Shells," *Triquarterly*, Fall 1986: 135-147; "The Baobab," *Black Warrior Review*, Fall 1987: 21-36; "Bossboy and the Wild West," *The Antioch Review*, Winter 1986: 88-104; "Cropped," *The Literary Review*, Fall 1986: 33-40; "A Walk Down the Beach," *Sonora Review*, Spring 1987: 42-55; "What They See," *Nimrod*, Fall 1985: 13-16.

Library of Congress Cataloging-in-Publication Data

Drew, Eileen, 1957–
    Blue taxis : stories about Africa / by Eileen Drew : foreword by
Rosellen Brown : designed and illustrated by R.W. Scholes.
        p.   cm.
    ISBN 0-915943-41-7 : $9.95
    1. Africa—Fiction.   I. Title.
PS3554.R438B55   1989
813'.54—dc20   89-12595
                                                                              CIP

For Lance

Foreword

Every book makes its own shape in the mind, a vague configuration that lingers like the memory of a painting, distinct against white space. Flaubert even wrote about the color a book made in his imagination — one of his novels was purple in his mind, and *Madame Bovary* began, he said, as an attempt only to render the color gray, village life as the exact dismal shade of "a woodlouse's existence." (He went so far as to say that Emma herself was an afterthought: she was, at first, to have been "a chaste old maid"!)

When I read a batch of promising manuscripts, as I have just done for Milkweed Editions' National Fiction Prize, one of the things I realize I am looking for—this is always, of course, after the fact; it is a retrospective view I'm hardly conscious of at first reading—is a vivid combination of elements, shape and color as they are translated in words. I am searching for a clear profile, an apprehension of a personality so assertive that I can see it and hear it when I turn away from the page. For all its intelligence, a great deal of very good work just doesn't bulk up that way; though it may speak in a recognizable voice, it doesn't cut its shape in the imagination, and so, though the words go down easily enough in the reading, they self-destruct in the memory.

Eileen Drew's *Blue Taxis* defines its own space very vividly, and in the act of doing so it articulates layer on layer of sociological and political wisdom. My first apprehension of the book, in fact, was literally spatial. When I finished reading these stories and closed my eyes, figuratively speaking, what I saw were primarily outdoor spaces, light-struck, under a wide African sky: browning savannah, cooling air, a slow sinuous river, village courtyards. Drew is not smitten with a romantic view of the veldt, a desire to paint the kind of sweeping vistas that so bedazzled film audiences in Hollywood's construction of *Out of Africa*, those graceful, grazing lions, the little oases of trees, all of it under a haze of swelling music. In fact she doesn't write much atmospheric description at all. For one thing, her Africa is not particularly beautiful—it tends far more toward dusty villages and the provincial streets plied by the blue taxis of the title story, the ground "packed dense, pitted and scattered with rubble."

It is no coincidence that the stories tend most often to take place out-of-doors under a tropical sky, and yet are not "about" the Beauty That is Africa. The people in Drew's stories do not often enter each other's houses, and here we discover a simple-sounding fact that defines her terrain—the need to meet and conduct their business in natural light is a result of the social distinctions between her characters. Except that it is perhaps too artlessly direct, the book could really have been called *Insiders and Outsiders*, which measures physical, psychological and, most significantly, political distances. These Africans and Americans, though sometimes friends or associates, are not exactly the kind of friends who visit comfortably and incessantly as equals in each other's houses.

Her Americans are, with a few exceptions, too smart to think they "belong" in this Africa of the new colonialism of the Peace Corps and of business and diplomatic dealings. But it is hard for them, and bitterly discouraging, to remember all the time how wide the gap is between what they see and what their hosts see. Here a teacher-volunteer is cannily understood by an African schoolgirl to be a "one-year missionary without a church" (and is that far from the truth?). To another young African, a wristwatch looks like high technology; it is a challenge to imagine the "ethical system of those who wore coats," to learn to tolerate ice in a glass. An upwardly-mobile young man drinks American whiskey instead of palm wine, but, for most, America is "a vast pale splotch" on the map and the root-word of "white" is intended for animals, not for people.

In one of Drew's best stories, "Ancient Shells," both funny and profoundly disquieting, we see the American teacher-volunteer through the eyes of a teenage girl, Ruzi, whose cynicism far outruns anything the disillusioned teacher could dream up. She understands, for example, that "girls go to school so bachelor teachers don't have to get married"—they can't, because the government pays them so badly. "We go to school so our dowries will be high, so our fathers will be rich.

And since we can't marry until we finish," there's nothing to stop teachers from exacting sexual payment for passing grades. It is a closed economy in which girls like Ruzi are small change, and though she recognizes her situation, the idea of trying to do anything about it is both preposterous and threatening to her. When Ruzi decides that the innocent, hopeful "Miss" isn't intelligent enough to be a teacher, we see with wonderful clarity what Miss looks like to her, and how right she is (bothersome moral questions aside) for her own purposes. And yet, and yet . . . even Ruzi is bitter in the lockstep rotation through the way things are. "Ancient Shells" is a story that runs in a perfect circle, connecting the flawed knowledge of the insider with the flawed knowledge of the outsider, trapping the reader disturbingly inside the circle.

Yet change, or the hunger for change, if it is not at the center of these stories, is right off to the side of every one of them. Although many would be satisfied to "own a car and a machine to wash clothes," the most enterprising young Africans are desperate to escape to the U.S. (and fail, of course, because escape is all luck and connections, not to mention money), or arrive to become absurdities—one man creates fast food hit, in a "bright and hostile" suburb, called the "Baobab Burger" after the African tree of that name. Or a young, embittered rider in the blue taxi of the title story threatens and humiliates a diplomat's daughter, shouting at her, "Always without worries . . . so high in your skyscrapers and airplanes, your homes like botanical gardens . . . You think nothing can happen here because you are white . . . You never get our problems, there's nothing can touch that watery skin," while at home her father is undergoing the parallel, if more polite, humiliation of having his residence searched for wiretapping equipment. (This is another of the stories where action is located almost solely out-of-doors, between the tennis court where the adolescent narrator conducts a discreet crush on a laconic black tennis instructor—hardly a candidate for her parlor—and the suddenly dangerous street where she is accosted by the man in the taxi whose frustration even she, at the beginning of her awakening to the world, can almost sympathize with.)

And, in "A Walk Down the Beach," revolution has finally broken out, but this time it will bring about more than political change: the need for foreigners to leave the country is the occasion for an inhibited, unhappily married consul's wife to be delivered from her private misery. Her husband is a man who habitually rubs his hands together "as if everything had just been resolved," but Alice's life is less and less resolved. Here, as in the best of *Blue Taxis*, we see again the delicate balance between the insider's and the outsider's view of Africa, but this time we are shown the subtle gradations even of *not* belonging: the doctor casually dispenses pills because "drugging wives when things got tense was apparently normal procedure," especially for the women who drag along behind their Foreign Service officer husbands. There are veteran expatriates among them but Alice is not one; she is still rubbed raw by her terror of dirt, of native contamination, of demands too great for her anxious hold on motherhood, wifehood, personhood. And as she and her daughter escape down the beach, fleeing the encroaching unrest—this is Guinea in the '60s—they "try to look European" rather than American, yet another distinction among aliens: outsider-ness is a finely graded scale.

But everything in Eileen Drew's fascinating book is fine-grained. She is a lucid and broadly sympathetic observer, gifted with a light touch and a sense of the impossibly painful (yet, often, absurdly funny) ironies that manipulate racial, national and tribal institutions and the people caught in their gears. Yet there is nothing didactic about her vision. These are stories without villains; everyone, no matter how well-intentioned, is the victim of an untenable situation.

Blue Taxis reads like a novel in the sense that, viewed from a step or two back from their particulars, the individual characters and their situations cohere; the protagonist turns out to be the continent of Africa itself. Like the stories of Norman Rush, or the early work of Paul Theroux—visitors all to the unyielding complexities of African village life—Eileen Drew's stories give us an unforgettable lesson in relativism, pragmatism, realism—and also in the infinity of particular, loving attachments and gratifications of a life lived open-eyed in that delicate balance.

—Rosellen Brown

BLUE TAXIS

Blue Taxis

Bossboy
and the
Wild West

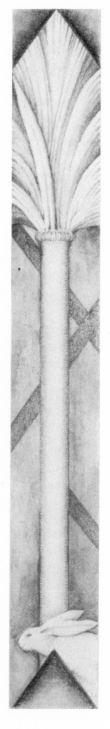

I start with Bossboy. Someone asks how it was, what Africa was like. People wait for Africa summed up. And I can't talk about the heat between skin touching.

The New York apartment is cold, barely furnished so far. Winter seeps in through the window. Alone while Graham meets with loan officers to set our plans in motion, I try out answers. A part of me needs shedding before I can step back into America, into Fifth Avenue's skirts and boots.

I start with Bossboy in Semba City. I was walking home from the American library where I worked mornings. I knew him the minute I turned onto my dirt street.

He was taller, his shoulders dense and cheekbones solid, the fuzz around his mouth beginning a sparse African beard. In this boy's dark face, however, I saw also the child masked in costume paint, the wobbly eyes five years younger. Even now, they won't let go.

"Miss Jane," he said, shaking my hand hard. "You remember me!"

Although he smelled of sweat, his hand was dry. He looked stylish and frantic, his flared trousers streaked with dried mud, torn at one knee. Missing buttons, his shirt flapped. Scratches crisscrossed his bare feet; blood had scabbed around the toenails.

Semban hospitality said I couldn't ask why he'd come or imply I knew he needed help. But I could hurry him inside to eat and drink, so he'd relax and talk.

He kept to the edges, stopping at the threshold until coaxed to sit, then perching on the bamboo rim of a chair, afraid of the cushion. "I'm sorry, I'm dirty," he said.

And he began to explain before I could offer a glass of water. "I walked from the river, down by Mbemba, you know Kulunsi?"

He was talking about a military camp near a town three hundred kilometers away.

After I nodded, he went on. "I had to keep off the paved road to hide from the police. So I came up the village roads, asking one person and another which way. Some were good and gave me food. But the first two days I had to get through forest with no machete."

"But why were you hiding from the police?"

"They took me for military service. In Kibundu they took me, tied me in the truck, and tore my identity card. Without my card I can be thrown in prison. But that training camp is like prison. Sleeping on the floor. No food. One man was so sick he never moved, but he told me, 'Go!' "

Bossboy spoke quietly, too quietly. His temples jumped as he swallowed. He said he had nowhere to go; the police would know him in his town, Kibundu. But he could work very hard. Could I get him a special work card? He nearly vibrated with tension, as if he might rush off looking for a broom.

"It'll be fine, we'll do something," I said. I didn't know what. Graham and I were leaving. "Did you know we're leaving Semba?" I asked.

Then his chin stuck forward and his eyes glazed. "Like Max."

This stiff expression was a mature version of the face I remember so well from Max's goodbye party, the cowboy party in Kibundu. That bush face: a child shocked but too needy to be angry, still full of hope, a tiny, yearning look streaked blue, yellow and red in mock war paint.

Bossboy was the child who cooked and cleaned for Max, my fellow American teacher at Kibundu Secondary School. Haphazardly paired by AfricEd to "share the challenge," Max and I grew during our two-year contracts to be as familiar and at odds as siblings.

From day one, though, Max made me laugh. I was still unpacking, knocking down cobwebs, when he appeared at my bungalow door in an old safari helmet with a mosquito net falling to his shoulders.

"Cocktail hour, I believe," he said, holding out a liter bottle of Semban beer. "The principal left a case in my house, a gesture of welcome."

Bossboy was on Max's heels already, a waist-high shadow carrying the tray and glasses, his round, curious eyes bulging.

Max swept off his hat, and I noted the short, prickly hair that would be blond if clean, the thick neck and lumpy nose. His fingers were stubby but moved quickly, sure of objects. Scuffing in flip-flops across the floor, he set the bottle down, hat on top.

I always think of Max as a voice booming with his body stumbling behind, with his little black boy staring. Bossboy saw everything and he was smart. Max had nicknamed him Bossboy because he could boss traders into good prices, Max's students into cleaning rabbit cages, even Max himself into learning dialect. "What do you call a hand?" Bossboy would ask. "What is a house?"

Bossboy as an adolescent fugitive of the military did not surprise me. A few of my Kibundu students had disappeared. For a day or so the teachers would wag their heads, clucking tongues and muttering about the army, the president—"Our Pilot," the sad state of Semba. No one discussed, just muttered. Joseph, the philosophy teacher, finally explained.

I spent my first year asking questions and Joseph, more than anyone, answered. Then he wanted to learn about America. He was handsome, brown fingers diagramming logic in the air, his great flat forehead hooding eyes drawn to horizons. Even inside he'd turn his head to a window, stare away, answering, asking. We played chess—he actually taught me because he thought my

Western mind would offer him authentic competition. I lost always; I'd avoided chess for a reason. Chess and law school, although my parents had not given up goading.

Joseph was built too well for a philosopher, but then Africans were muscular, toughened as children by carrying water and hoeing fields. I teased him, when we got to be lovers, that he was all wrong for America. Too athletic to be an intellectual, too smart for physical labor. He dreamed anyway of living in the big, rich States.

Max had his own information sources. We tended to turn to African friends before we turned to each other. Then, in order to compare notes, we excused what we didn't like about each other, us against them. I ignored his steady stream of languid whores. Often I dropped in at his house to find some prettily disheveled woman stirring beans while Bossboy chopped onions or cleaned rice. I'd leave.

Joseph would laugh, if he were with me. "And why can't you cook?" he'd ask.

"Won't," I'd say, "won't."

No Kibundan women taught; the teacher wives I'd met talked babies and gossip and never went out. So I turned to Joseph, and it was he who cured my initial confusion, who taught me how Semba worked. He explained about the missing students.

After one kid disappeared from school, Joseph and I sat on my porch plodding through a game of chess, talking more than playing, and I learned that the president's army kidnapped teenagers to make them police because no one volunteered. No one volunteered because the troops were never paid. Paradoxically, police wielded power mainly because they were criminals licensed with M-16s to steal their livelihoods.

How could this be? Our Pilot was a charismatic dictator with special links to the sky and to the afterworld. He seemed constantly in the air between regions. Accompanied by a whole air battalion he roared unexpectedly into cities, keeping dissenters on their toes. To his credit, he'd kept peace among tribes for twenty years.

"But why don't you do something?" I asked Joseph. "How can a whole country stand for that? How can you just sit there?"

He explained that the Pilot's power rested as much in Semban superstition as in the military machine.

"For example," he enunciated, waving a pawn over the board. "A village man will tell you that the Pilot has fetishes. If you plan an assassination or coup, you die. Just like that." He had opened his fingers, dropping the pawn. "The Pilot knows, they will say."

Suddenly I saw Joseph as Semban, passive, waiting for curses and cures, for me to spirit him to America. The pawn rolled in a circle near my heel.

"I hate chess," I said. "I concede." I did not want to be his miracle.

Bossboy was desolate yet dignified after he heard Graham and I were soon to be in the States; I realized he had hoped to work for us. He agreed to be our guest. Inspecting rips and scabs, he wondered when Graham would arrive; he wanted to be clean and sharp, as if for an interview. Our house worker, Sunday, helped me set out leftovers—rice, fish, cake, whatever the refrigerator offered—and I watched Bossboy eat. He ate less desperately than methodically, wiping the dishes clean with bread, licking his fingers.

I sipped a glass of beer, my usual lunch. Normally, afternoons were dead. Sometimes I had two beers. Sometimes I went to *Best Legs*, Graham's store, and got in the way.

Boredom was why we were leaving. We had agreed our brains were stalling. Life was easy and cheap, but we were missing the future; nothing was changing in Semba. I wanted to see a computer.

I showed Bossboy the guest room and shower; he could rest a few hours. Sunday went off to borrow clothes from a nephew. Then I began to sort old letters for Max's most recent address. I tried to avoid my mother's handwriting; it conjured a hoarse voice quizzing, "But aren't they all black? Do they have soap?"

On one card from Tokyo, Max had scrawled, "Teaching jobs abound. Money, too. Might stay." I fingered the frayed corners. Inherently indefinite, Max would never know what was coming. He didn't want or need to know. No address would be sure; he'd be impossible to track. And if I did find him, what then? He'd already tired of his father game, had probably never written to Bossboy.

I saw again Bossboy's antelope eyes, the stun of desertion. I couldn't leave Semba like that. Max was rootless, vagabond, a slob. My challenge had materialized, it seemed: three dimensions, flesh and blood — Bossboy. I restacked the miscellaneous envelopes neatly, picturing Bossboy mature and tidy, and then Graham.

Funny how Graham inspired self-consciousness. I needed that. When we met he was conspicuously exuberant; a crazy American without a contract, he was politically unencumbered. He came to Africa to enjoy making a living, not to develop the third world. He had no problem with that.

At the time, Kibundu was a dim cocoon of failure paralyzing me. Graham oxidized my Africa. Westerners there were usually institutionalized, belonging to government, church or corporation. Graham belonged to himself. His goal was to supply, on a small scale, what Sembans needed. He would take people aside, one at a time. "Tell me," he'd say, cocking his head to imply secrecy, "what do you need? What can't you buy?"

The day he swooped into the back yard of *Bobo's Urban World*, the teachers were on strike. Our wood table was soggy with the accumulated sweat of beer bottles. Cards creased and smeared by dusty fingers lay scattered in abandoned hands. Even Bossboy, dwarfed in his own chair beside Max, slumped precariously, dozing mid-air. Joseph had secured my pack of cigarettes in the crook of a branch within his reach, high and dry. This table was strike headquarters; sheltered by the acacia, we idled.

Teachers struck at random, by town or by school; there was no regional or national organization. They wanted money: salaries, when they did arrive, were insufficient. As government employees the teachers, like the police, missed pay when central funds ran dry.

Max and I were supposed to be apolitical; after all, the Pilot was an American ally. The U.S. got copper and cobalt, Semba got arms. But each day that the students found no teachers, they cut school. Confronted with empty classrooms, Max and I decided from the first strike to support the teachers. We bought the beer. Since our healthy salaries were secured by AfricEd, we bought until we got low and everyone voted to return to work.

Early on, before this pattern established itself, Max held a vote at Bobo's about beer money. He stood, feet wide apart, unkempt as a jungle. Shirt dotted with holes, dingy hair hiding watery eyes, unshaven, he swayed beside the acacia, waving the gritty fingernails I kept asking him to cut. Should Max and I simply distribute our cash so some could buy food instead of beer?

Solemnly, trying to keep secret ballots from sopping up the ubiquitous condensation, the eight teachers and school secretary penned "No" behind half-full glasses. Our money was ours to do with what we wanted, they agreed, knowing we'd buy beer.

By the third strike of my second year, I'd given away my syllabus to a market lady who was always pestering me for scrap paper to wrap produce. My students would never get beyond chapter one.

This particular afternoon was waning, the acacia drooping nearly onto the table. I felt acutely that Bobo's building was crumbling, speck by speck, into the red dirt ground. A goat brayed from over the fence. We'd decided to go back to work next week. Beer money was waning. I was waning.

At the height of a torpor interrupted only by intermittent W.C. trips, during this inertia of bloated bellies and smoky lungs and melting brains, the afternoon zipped to attention. A sturdy white man stood at Bobo's back door, facing us, the only customers.

Bobo's smiling face appeared over the stranger's shoulder. "Ice," I kept hearing. The white arms pumped angularly, shaping something invisible. "Ice."

"Hello!" shouted Ngongo, the secretary, waving. He always felt it his business to clear things up. Too late: the figures had disappeared, leaving a dark hole gaping in the lime green facade.

"You see," I said. "A hallucination. No ice."

"Beer!" shouted Ngongo.

"No more beer," said Max. "Ice."

Little Bossboy was twisting, looking from the door to Max. The religion teacher, whose seven-syllabled name I always remembered incorrectly, Matutezulwa, or Matetelewazo, said, "But what about this ice?"

Max played the messiah, cherry lips clarifying through a beneficent smile. "Cold, hard, frozen, winter. My friends, ice chills the fever. In the north are whole continents of ice. The air is so cold you need"—and here he paused for emphasis—"coats!"

"Coats," repeated Joseph, imagining, no doubt, the ethical system of those who wore coats, imagining himself in one.

Yala, who taught physics, was not fooled. "Come now, we all know ice. You Europeans put little boxes of ice in drinks, we've seen this in films. And no one can live in Antarctica. Put on coats, you still die. Why ice?"

"Americans," I said. "Not Europeans."

"Antarctica is south," said Pangi. He taught geography and history. "Third form just learned that."

The man reappeared cradling something in his arms. As he neared at an unseasonal trot, dust puffing at his feet, I recognized a bottle neck sticking out of an ice bucket.

Max droned on. "And, my friends, ice chills the beer."

As the pale hands deposited the bucket on the table, all talking stopped. The stranger stood tall, arms folded, ignoring the sun. His watch glinted. The only sweat I saw was around his mouth. He shaved. He smiled at everyone. His dark hair looked as if he had washed it that morning. He smiled at me. At me in my wrinkled dress with the marigolds faded to ghosts, me with my hair dripping, my everything awful.

My entropic state was partly due to my attempt to discourage Joseph, still hopeful after my decision, six months earlier, to kick him out of my bedroom. Smug and patient, he couldn't believe a female could say no. It was cultural, of course. He was superior, he took away my cigarettes and stuck them in tree branches as if I couldn't take care of them myself.

We formed a circle of heads and peered into the container as Max continued in his messianic way, "A Western luxury here, an ice *bucket*. To keep the beer cold, the bottle from perspiring." He pressed his thumb against the frosty glass, leaving an imprint. Joseph did the same. One by one, the others touched the bottle.

"Sit, my friend. Tell us," said Ngongo, taking advantage of Max's silence.

The man sat then in one of the metal patio chairs Bobo was suddenly holding. Bobo sat in the other, beaming. Bobo was huge and silent. He ran his club telepathically, it seemed; you never saw him move but things got done. Beer arrived, a record got flipped.

Bobo recited our names while we took turns shaking the calm, firm hand. Bossboy met solemnly the prospect of the extended white palm, shaking with his whole arm. Bobo said Max and I were from, respectively, New Jersey Village and California Village. Pangi grimaced.

Graham, Bobo explained, was an "ice man" from California Village. "This California," Bobo asked me, "is a very large village?"

"State," Pangi cut in. "Like a region, like East Semba."

"I'm starting a business," said Graham.

We all sat forward.

"Kibundu is my test market. If it works here I'll start in Semba City. You're all urbanized, educated, sophisticated. Lots of schools and commerce here."

A satellite town three hours from the city, Kibundu was not much more than peeling paint and starving teachers. Unpaid sophisticates.

"And how much is this ice?" asked Ngongo. He liked expenses; he kept a file of imaginary school budgets in case money ever came. I gave him my calculator when I left Kibundu.

"A few cents extra per bottle of beer," Graham told us with clipped eloquence. He sounded as if he'd lived in England. To each club he'd rent a large, non-electric cooler, and then deliver the ice daily from his ice factory. Clubs in towns like Kibundu had the electric refrigeration to chill beer but no way to make ice. Each club would have to buy the ice buckets.

Bobo was smiling graciously, hands hidden in his lap amid the folds of his traditional robes.

"The first month, though, I'll supply everything to the owners free." Bobo nodded.

Meanwhile the bottle in its metallic armor stood waiting, fingerprints expanding, a lone boat in a puddle.

"So let's try this beer," said the religion teacher, elbows on wide knees.

"Wait," said Graham, crossing his legs as if we were at a tropical resort. "Wait and see how long it stays cold."

We eyed the bottle. Minutes passed. The frost ignored our thirst, refusing to melt.

"Perhaps we should put it in the sun," suggested Joseph.

Max laughed.

"I don't see why we are waiting," Joseph insisted. "I don't see the purpose of this ice. Beer comes to the table, we drink."

Of course, he was right. Sembans did not wait for their beer to warm.

"However," started Max. He'd gone serious again. "With ice there is no hurry. You don't have to immediately guzzle."

"I've had this idea ever since I travelled here a few years ago," Graham agreed. "Africa needs ice. You think?" He looked from Max to me.

"I need ice," said Max laboriously. "Do you need ice?" He looked at our teacher friends, one by one, resting his gaze a few seconds on each. Compared to Graham, Max operated like an old man. I had an urge to grab his bristly chin and push his gaze faster.

At Bossboy he stopped his visual inquiry and grinned. "You need ice, Bossboy, here—." Max scooped a few cubes from the bucket and licked one, handing the rest to Bossboy. "Like this, try."

Bossboy juggled the ice. He laughed, put a whole cube in his mouth, spat it out. "That's cold!" he panted.

Max retrieved some of Bossboy's ice and planted it on top of the boy's head. "Don't move," ordered Max, and Bossboy sat happily dripping, thrilled while we all shouted and clapped.

Bobo finally got the sign to pour. Each glass got a few fingers, even Bobo's and Graham's, which I hadn't seen arrive. But Graham placed his glass in front of Bossboy, whose Coke bottle was empty. Bossboy wiped his wet face.

"To ice," said Max.

We gulped. I licked my lips, and Graham smiled.

The cowboy party was Max's idea, a grand finale to our two years in Kibundu. Our contracts fulfilled, Max was embarking on a worldwide odyssey; I was staying in Semba with Graham. The party money came from Max's rabbit project. He'd sent proposals all over Bashushi and amassed funds, mostly from A.I.D. and the Catholic mission, to keep the rabbits procreating. The students ate them. That was the point: the rabbits supplied a cheap food source for the school. Max had proposed expenses for cage upkeep and rabbit food. Actually the rabbits lived on scraps and weeds and students cleaned the cages as part of physical education. So when the money came he appointed Ngongo to draw up the real budget.

One afternoon at Max's, Ngongo, treasurer of "Kibundu Rabbit Nursery," crouched gleefully over my calculator, drawing columns and figures. He'd already entered "1,000" next to "preliminary feed stock." That was for the cowboy party.

Using a packed trunk for a table, Max and I figured the party budget. "Ice," I wrote, "gratis."

Graham was holding onto his ice machines just for the party. He'd already found a buyer, a South African meat importer who had more use than Semban beer drinkers for ice. Bobo's was the only club where Graham had broken even.

Doodling, I imagined myself busy in Semba City, working for someone air-conditioned, entertaining Semban friends in Graham's air-conditioned apartment, taking hot showers, driving an air-conditioned car. Graham was up there trying to figure out what, this time, Sembans really did need. His latest brainstorm was a huge coil in a barrel to heat water electrically. "I'll have one rigged up by the time you get there," he'd said a few days before. He'd been staying at my moldy teacher's bungalow during his frequent visits to Kibundu, and now I would be sharing his city place. I was not going to California. I was not going back to my parents who kept trying to extract me from the heart of darkness and tuck me into law school.

"Bossboy!" shouted Max as the child entered holding a broom upright with both hands so it towered like a substitute dance partner. He stopped, velvety eyes on Max.

But Max was talking to Ngongo. "Don't forget a salary for Bossboy! He's got to be paid to keep those students sweeping rabbit poop and gathering grass. A good salary, for a good worker!"

Bossboy smiled at the broom bristles as if blushing, but his skin stayed brown. Industrious, not yet sad, he pumped the tall broom back and forth, tough fingers gripping the handle down near the base so the tip swung wildly way above his bent back.

"Where did that broom come from?" I asked Max.

"Found it yesterday, going through a closet. It's been in this house forever, from some missionary, I guess. I hope I, too, can leave such a distinguished symbol for posterity."

I thought of his women, and couldn't resist. "Posterity? I guess you *are* leaving yourself behind."

"Not funny. I, at least, never accumulated the mass of glittering objects in your abode. Tins in every corner."

"All consumables. Of which *you* have done the major consuming."

We were referring to the Western goodies Graham had been supplying — orange drink powder, sardines, tubes of shampoo, Marlboros. The Johnnie Walker I'd given unopened to Max.

Bossboy was jerking across the floor, mouth open, struggling with the white man's broom.

Max got up, disappeared down the hall, and returned with the African-style broom, long bristled with a short handle. "Use this one," he said to Bossboy. Max bent and gave a huge sweep. Dust scattered. "Even for me," Max said, "this one is better."

Haltingly, never sure when Max was joking, Bossboy began to swing the long bristles, looking more at Max than at the floor.

"Excellent," said Max.

Satisfied, Bossboy swished across the room, drowning out the plastic punch of Ngongo's fingers on the calculator.

We addressed the invitations to Wild West characters, names we invented: Black Cloud Joseph, Quickcount Ngongo, Bobo Sitting Bull. Max was Town Sheriff. I was Whispering Weed.

Miracle Man Graham brought some theater make-up from Semba City, and everyone's face got painted. I did Bossboy's with elaborate squiggles and white around his eyes so they looked even bigger than usual. He was Minnehaha. He distributed the chicken feathers for headdresses.

The square dancing was a hit. Max the Town Sheriff called the steps as Semban high life blared. Bossboy, Graham, Ngongo, and I demonstrated, and before long the floor was so crowded the dance degenerated into human bumper cars. Then Sheriff Max put on some "bang-your-head-against-the-wall-music," as he called it, and we demonstrated the pogo. New dances became a theme that evening, and, hours later after beer had run out, people were doing the "ice walk," balancing the last cubes on heads while lifting knees rhythmically. By that point Sheriff Max was in war paint and feathers even though he wasn't Indian because, he was telling everyone, he was cross-cultural. I was telling the story of Whispering Weed.

Bossboy and I sat outside in the miniature *paillotte*, in Max's front yard. Not the popular outdoor spot Max had envisioned, the low ceiling drooped between bamboo poles. Bossboy had supervised the round hut's construction the year before and then no one had used it after the first week. The thatch bench and walls were scratchy; the urbanized teachers scorned the mock village architecture. Still, the wall stopped about four feet high so that you got a nice open-air view when seated. I liked the breeze. Over music thudding from the house a chorus of insects clicked and surged.

Minnehaha Bossboy wanted his face repainted. He'd come out on Max's porch to stand blinded by the sudden night, searching, hands dangling apart from his body, suspended in indecision.

"Jane?" he called, peering in the direction of the *paillotte*.

"Yes, Minnehaha," I said, "come and sit."

At the entrance, an open space in the round wall, he stopped. "I saw in the mirror my face is bad now. Can you fix it?"

"Sure, we'll go back to the house in a minute." I lured him in with my Coke.

Across from me on the bamboo bench, he blended into the gloomy interior.

"I'm rooted here, but I don't belong," I said. "Like a weed, you know?"

"Yes, Jane." The Coke can glinted. Aside from that he was featureless but full of voice.

"Whispering Weed," I corrected. "A weed, a plant that grows by itself where another type is supposed to. *Sundi ko*, bad grass." I translated, literally, from his dialect.

"Eh, you speak *Ligongo!*"

"Not so well. Not like you taught Max."

Bossboy was silent, thinking, I guessed, about Max. Then the voice poked out stark and tiny as a needle. "Then why, Jane, why does he leave me?"

I could feel how taut he must look trying not to cry: color streaks zigzagging across a face crumpled and trembling. He was brimming with feeling, too small to contain his sudden vision of Max gone. Tragedy filled the *paillotte*, rose up and spilled over the wall, smearing the enormous night. He was so sad he put out the stars, I thought, until I remembered the *paillotte* roof.

I didn't know what to say. I hadn't thought; I wondered if Max had. He'd been Bossboy's idol. Max had made Bossboy big. Max was leaving Bossboy behind.

Of course, he had to. How could Max drag a kid around the globe? But Bossboy had believed in magic.

I don't remember how I answered Bossboy in the *paillotte*. Maybe I explained how Max had no choice, how we were both white shmucks with no power who would help if we could.

I do remember what rescued me from the flooded *paillotte*: a dance chain emerging from the house. About ten people followed Ngongo, hands on the waist of the person ahead, and jerked to the music, hooting and laughing around the corner of the house.

"That one a new dance, Jane?" asked Bossboy.

The shouts faded as they rounded the back, and then got louder again on the third side, as they neared the front.

"The *paillotte*!" we heard as they appeared, headed straight for us. "Jaaane!"

I recognized Joseph's voice and remembered a scene. The very day we'd met Graham at Bobo's we had all crowded into Graham's Land Rover, piling on top of freezers, and he chauffeured us home. Max sat up front with Graham while I was wedged between Joseph and Pangi. Joseph always had to be right beside me. Everyone wanted him there but me.

But when we pulled up at my house and Joseph started to follow me out the door, I lost patience. "No!" I stage whispered. "Go home!" The others in the back eyed me with amusement. Recalcitrant females made them laugh. I slipped out and swung shut the door in Joseph's face. Through the dusty window I saw his palms, fingers spread, blocking the door, blocking this odd phenomenon. His face, slack and drunk, registered amazement. Angry, I felt sorry, then angry because I felt sorry. That's why I hadn't got rid of him; I felt sorry.

And here he was at the goodbye party, still calling my name, in a human caterpillar bumping toward the *paillotte*. Bossboy and I hooked on and jiggled across the lawn to the house. The floor was slick with puddles of melted ice. Under the kitchen light I painted triangles and circles all over Bossboy's face while he stood solid. "Put a smile," he begged, and I did, in yellow.

The next time I saw him, on the empty dance floor, he had the tall broom. Psychedelic, haunted, he was like a child witch about to fly away. But instead he used the broom to push water from the puddles out the door. Everyone looked. He was great.

Graham was dancing alone in the corner. In just several months he'd gone African. He danced where and when it felt good. And he'd slowed. Funny, I liked him all the more. His hips swung gently, his feet inching, head tilted. Very African.

Sitting near the door for the cool air, I watched the water trickle past. Graham danced toward the room's center, then up behind Bossboy. As he turned from the door to retrace his steps, Bossboy faced Graham.

"What do you need?" I heard Graham ask. "I haven't asked you yet." He twirled a circle and repeated the words as if they were part of the dance. "What do you need?"

Bossboy, surreal, armed with the broom, stared. He watched Graham twirl again, eyes on the flared legs of Graham's faded pants.

"Blue jeans," Bossboy answered through his yellow grin.

So by the time Graham arrived to find the fugitive Bossboy in our living room, I'd decided. Bossboy was my ticket to leave Africa with a clean conscience. In seven years I'd done nothing for any Semban; had I ever really tried? I wasn't sure. Bossboy had asked neither Max nor me for what he really wanted, for the real miracle: America. I would get Bossboy out.

Graham arrived damp and thirsty. Bossboy stood like a palm, narrow and balanced; until they met to shake hands briskly, Bossboy seemed taller.

"Zunai," he introduced himself, abandoning the child label. Then as I summarized his story, he sat leaning on his knees; composed and direct, he seemed less helpless.

Graham listened, wiping his face with a bandana pulled from his shirt pocket, accepting a gin and tonic from Sunday.

"How?" was his first response. I, of course, had not asked this practical question. My angle was more "why?" Or, "what does this mean?" You see why I had liked Joseph.

"Tell us, my friend," said Graham. "How did you escape?" More than curious, he was awed.

"These guards, they get drunk, go to sleep, so I went out the front gate, very very quietly."

"No fights, no hitting?"

Bossboy shook his head, flexing his scratched hands. "I climbed a tree and stayed for the next day, up very high, while they looked on the ground for me. I knew they can find you before you walk far enough away. So I waited until they stopped looking, then walked through the forest. I got very dirty." He brushed the seat cushion beside his legs. Nothing fell.

I had trouble fitting the day's earlier drama, Bossboy crawling from the forest, with this dignified young man. Was this new self-assurance the result of his rest, or of his audience with Graham? With me Bossboy had, perhaps, allowed himself anxiety.

Or maybe he was shrewd, playing for my sympathy as opposed to Graham's respect. Maybe he was conning me, as Joseph had.

"So it's easy to escape?" Graham asked. "I mean, it's not really like prison."

"You can never go from prison."

I said, "He can go to prison now for leaving that camp, though. He has no papers."

"We'll fix you up," said Graham.

We did all we could. I kept my rescue plan a secret from Bossboy so as not to disappoint, in case things went wrong. I didn't want to start him hoping. And I knew Graham would resist.

He was still all good looks and efficiency, purely generous, aware of his limits. His power was a blend of luck and charisma — he'd gambled his small inheritance on African business until we were scrambling for the price of airfare out, but he knew people. Intent on the I.D. card, he spent hours in government offices looking for the right strings to pull.

The week Bossboy lived with us the house was immaculate, the floor slippery as ice, the long threads fringing the rug ridiculously even. Sunday even complained of wasted soap. Yet they got along; Sunday didn't mind when Bossboy ignored my requests to quit working and act like a guest.

Nights I lobbied for Bossboy's move to America.

"Zunai," Graham would say, "not Bossboy." He was realistic; we couldn't afford another ticket, nor the palm-greasing for an exit visa. What would we do with him in New York?

I had worked out the money problem. I would wire my parents, who were dying to pay my fare to the States, and use the extra funds for Bossboy. My parents' help had always required behavior modification from me—a car if I quit smoking, Europe if I dropped a boyfriend—and my policy had been, no deal. This time I would play dirty.

"You're mixed up," Graham said one night. "You're striking out at guilt. Why can't you just be what you are? You're fine, you don't have to be a savior or a hotshot professional."

"But, poor Bossboy."

"He's a big boy, Jane, he got himself out of that police camp." Graham's hand closed on mine, and, eyes closed, I felt all of me inside his gentle fist. I imagined the air-conditioner's chugging as his heartbeat, echoing from a giant chest, distant as the ceiling.

The next morning Bossboy was to apply for his special I.D. card that would exempt him from military service. Graham had set it up. Bossboy was oddly polite over coffee, I assumed because he was grateful.

We were alone; Graham always left early. I noticed Bossboy had shaved the fuzz from his upper lip. As he raised his cup, Graham's watch gleamed.

"You look very respectable," I said. "You're borrowing that watch?"

Bossboy smiled, turning his wrist. "It's Graham's gift. To be on time for my meeting today. And he said it would run always, no winding, and here is the date." Bossboy pointed. "Eh, if I could see the motor!" This was more than a toy to him, more than magic. This was intricate technology. I realized I knew nothing of him, and asked what he liked to study.

"Engineering. Maybe aeronautics." That answer made him thoughtful. Forehead creased, he asked, "Jane, where will I work with this card?"

"We'll find you something," I said. "Don't worry."

"When do you leave?"

"Not before we take care of you."

He looked down into his coffee. "In America, there are many jobs, aren't there?"

"You could get a job there," I said, picturing him three-piece suited, in a packed elevator, going up. "But first you'd have to go to school."

"University? Eh, if only. But I'll never go to America."

I asked why not; he explained. "A Semban has no way, no money, we are tiny ants. Only an American could take me." He looked straight at me with adult eyes, a man's eyes. They were not childishly helpless but challenging. I remembered Joseph. "Marry me," Joseph had said. "We'll go to America. We'll be rich and happy." And when I'd said no, "Marry me, then, as my friend. We can divorce in America."

Why did I owe Bossboy America? I wavered; maybe Graham was right. Of course he was right. I had no business trying to change the world, not even one man's life. I felt like a voodoo doll, old buried wood, bound stiff by earth.

After work Bossboy wasn't back. I drank beer, confronted my mother's letters, redefining her words inked like stabs into gold-embossed notepaper. Terms like "profession," "income," and "security" had always evoked her pushy ambitiousness, but they could mean any sort of life I chose. I didn't have to be either my parents' Jane or the exact opposite, mothered by a jungle.

Graham got home; Bossboy didn't. Sunday had no news. Bossboy didn't come and didn't come. We didn't sleep much. The next day he still hadn't returned. In his room his pairs of jeans from *Best Legs* were folded neatly, as usual. He never came for them.

We went down to Kulunsi Police Camp but they wouldn't let us in, not for any amount. Semba Prison was the same.

I'm glad Bossboy never knew of my plan. I liked finding Joseph's face in Bossboy's; I liked Bossboy defiant. That face was much easier to take than the needle voice in Max's *paillotte*.

I keep hearing it: "Why?" And each time I think of Bossboy I see that false yellow grin and the eyes scrunched shut while I, painting, drown them in white pools.

Ancient Shells

When Ruzi told her about Bola, Miss Christina said that ugly English word she never explained in class and turned bright as hibiscus. Miss was always damp around the mouth and where her hair met her forehead, wet so the strands which didn't reach the knot behind fell like tiny snakes on her cheeks. When angry she was like hibiscus after rain.

"Miss Tomato," the students would say to each other, but Ruzi never saw her that color. Ruzi saw the skin so transparent that blue veins laced the hands, climbed the arms. Veins zigzagged across Miss's feet too, swelling, then flattening with each step as she passed Ruzi's desk. Back in tenth-grade biology, Citizen Emolo had said everyone's blood was blue inside and came out red, yet Ruzi still imagined Miss bleeding blue, like ink.

The first day of school, the new teacher had walked into the senior class trembling on thin spider legs. "Christina James," she wrote on the board, and then, "Benton, New Jersey, U.S.A." The letters were loopy, the lines slanted. Her French was funny but no one laughed; a teacher could punish. Missionaries hit and Africans made you kneel in the sun. Mrs. Baxter, Ruzi's second-grade teacher at the church school, had taught silence. Noisy people had their knuckles pounded with a ruler. One girl's finger was broken.

Miss Christina wasn't with a mission, though. "Volunteer" appeared on the board as she explained the one-year contract. Ruzi understood then that this white was a one-year missionary without a church. Run by the state, Kundu Girls' School had no religion.

Even more puzzling, this woman was single. Old Mrs. Baxter's husband had died, but Miss, with skin smooth as clay, was too young to be alone.

And why would anyone leave rich America?

"Why not?" was the answer, when Nzuzi up front asked. "Africa might have something better than money."

Not in the bush, not at Kundu. The town was so quiet teachers refused to come; they all worked in Bossiville. The principal still hadn't found a math and physics teacher for this year. What was there to do?—No music, no bars, no cinemas, no life. Nothing but school.

"I like quiet," said Miss Christina. "It's clean."

Ruzi agreed, whites needed to slow down. The arm jerked across the blackboard, squeaking chalk. Pins were slipping from the knot of hair that looked crazy as a forest, with things hanging everywhere. If the hair were separated into eight parts, each knotted tightly to the scalp, Miss might be pretty. If she ate yams her face might get round, her nose less narrow. If she smiled.

Ruzi could braid beautifully. She'd learned on her mother and sisters, then her mother's friends and their daughters, fitting designs to each head's shape. She would memorize the newest Bossi styles on strangers in buses. Then, when Ruzi left the city for secondary school, her mother began going to the chic salons herself. Ruzi's technique became professional; each time she returned from Kundu for a holiday she could unravel the thread and pull apart the intricately woven tufts of her mother's stiff hair to redo the same style immediately on Mbengi, her sister. Mbengi strutted each experiment for days, refusing to carry anything on her head, until her mother yelled, "Lazy! Get away from the mirror and help Ruzi with the clothes. You're too pretty for your age."

Ruzi, though, would point to an empty stool on the patio and tell Mbengi about Kundu while her sister sat watching. Laundry was Mbengi's chore now, but Ruzi was happy with her arms wet to the elbows, dipping cloth after cloth into pails of sudsy water. Her two smaller sisters always squeezed into Mbengi's patch of shade and listened too, eyes wide at Ruzi's stories of dormitory rats, or of the red, sticky, rainy-season mud.

"Is it like the village?" asked the youngest once.

"No. All the buildings are cement, and there's electricity. It's school. I spend every morning in a classroom reading and writing, just like you will next year, except you'll come home every day. I wish I still did."

"Simon and Tuli like their school."

Her brothers were both smart. Even during vacations they read books, traded and then offered them to Ruzi, who laughed.

"They're boys," she said.

When her mother had told her she was going away to school, Ruzi had wailed, setting a pile of clean clothes on a kitchen chair. "I can stay here in Bossi, help you in the house," she said, wiping her eyes on the freshly folded sleeve of her father's shirt. "School isn't important for me, I'm barely passing."

Behind the stove her mother's face hung in steam. "Your father has decided. You will do better at Kundu with few distractions. He wants you to finish secondary school before you marry."

"For the dowry."

"For you also." The woody aroma of peanut stew somehow softened the voice. "Mintu wants an educated wife."

Folding the damp sleeve back on itself, Ruzi imagined the shirt was Mintu's, that school was finished and her father paid. They might live in a bush village after he finished studying agriculture at the university. Maybe even Abi village, where they'd met, where her father was born. According to him, Mintu would be a perfect husband, of a good clan from his own natal land. It was too early for arrangements, Mintu was still at secondary school, but everybody wanted them to marry. He wrote her letters. He visited when in Bossiville.

"But why can't I be educated here?"

"When do you study in this city? Already you think only of braiding hair. You'll get into trouble like all Bossi kids, drinking, dancing, smoking in the streets and missing school—stealing, even. You need discipline."

When Citizen Bola had said he'd raise her geography and history grades in exchange for evening meetings, his eyes tiny and dull as peppercorns had stung inside her stupid brain. Her last year was beginning badly, first the new white Miss and now this rat man. In the musty teachers' room Ruzi studied the few hairs on his pointy chin, the stick-out teeth and ears. Then the paint flaking off the wall around bookshelves of faded texts. Maps were stacked against the one window; opposite, the door was open wide. Bola seemed to belong to the mildew smell of a room shut all summer. Would his house smell the same?

"You must come at night, carefully," he said.

The arrangement was familiar. Ruzi knew several girls—all very pretty—who passed classes this way. Too poor to pay dowry, many teachers were bachelors. Before Miss Christina, the first woman teacher Ruzi had known at Kundu, the students were the only single females. Ruzi said nothing. If she could think like a boy, she could pass her classes herself. Bola had said once last year that if he were God he never would have created women, because they couldn't think. The whole class had shouted, pointing at Tusamba and Povi with the highest marks, and he'd said, "Because they can memorize. You can memorize, but you can't think."

Now he was saying, "Last year you failed my courses. If you fail again this year you won't have the cumulative points to graduate. I want to help you, but after three years I can see you'll never learn my lessons."

He spoke like her father, hands clasped on the table. There were no questions; the conference ended when his hand waved her away. He knew she would come.

38

That night, she thought of Mintu as she walked without a storm lamp across the school grounds; she was sneaking through Abi to meet Mintu under the baobab tree. Inside Bola's salon lit by a bare bulb in the ceiling, she pictured Mintu in the rat man's place as they sat sipping palm wine. In bed it was easier because she closed her eyes, and the wine made everything just fuzzy enough for Ruzi to imagine Mintu's wide, slow hands. During the next day's history quiz, though, she remembered quick claws scratching.

Miss Christina didn't smile at first. The night her hair was down, she smiled. Ruzi was on her way to Bola's, an empty pail in each hand so if anyone asked she could be fetching water from the tap near his house, when she saw Miss. Perched on the concrete washing block in her yard, she was talking to her neighbors' children.

Hiding Miss's shoulders, arms, and most of her face, the hair was a magic veil grown from nowhere; certainly it couldn't all have come from the knot behind her head. As Ruzi neared she saw strands rising and falling in the breezy dusk. Otherwise so still, Miss was odd as an ancestor. Away from the classroom, she was smiling, oblivious to the children's fingers touching.

Ruzi crossed the lawn and put the buckets down. "Your hair is very long," she said.

"Yes, it's too hot to wear down during the day."

"Doesn't it itch?"

"No. At home I always wore it like this."

"*Go away!*" Ruzi shouted at the kids, who ran to a safe spot under a tree. "You don't have to let them bother you."

"It's something different for them. I don't mind."

Like the children, Ruzi had to touch. She took a clump in her hand and began braiding; clumsy in sudden softness, her fingers plunged as if through water. She wondered if Miss knew her from class. Would she guess where Ruzi was going?

"No one can see your face like this."

"Everyone knows who I am. It's getting dark anyway."

Ancient Shells   39

"In America, then. You shouldn't hide your face. It looks dirty, dangerous. An open face is prettier."

"I could shave my head." Smiling, Miss seemed to be joking. At the tip Ruzi let go so the braid unraveled itself. How would she fasten such straight, slippery hair? She answered, "That's what our men do when their fathers die. Shave their heads."

Miss Christina shook her hair behind her shoulders with a wild jerk like a tail swishing. At night, then, Miss was happy, not hard as a plate, or electric bright with sweat.

Picking up her pails, Ruzi said, "I must go before it's dark."

Bola had said she could come at twilight, with the pails for an excuse. Ruzi hated the black nights eerie with owls, bats, possible snakes.

People knew anyway, even after only two weeks. Girls in the dorm had noticed her bed empty every few nights and asked who, until she got the "B" on the history quiz. Then she told them rat stories, that Bola slept under his bed because he was afraid of light, that he nibbled at his sheets. In class they made holes in the papers he returned and held them up to each other to show he'd been hungry.

Miss Christina probably didn't know. She didn't know anyone's name in class yet.

The next day, serious again, she called on Ruzi by pointing the usual stubby finger.

Miss never hit. By the end of September, English class was crazy; if people weren't talking all at once they were napping, heads resting on folded arms. As long as they spoke English, Miss didn't care. "If you want to fail, go to sleep," she said. "If you want to learn, listen." They were studying the conditional.

Cheating was the crime she hated, and her punishment was sneaky. After Ruzi found the angry red zero on her composition she looked for Miss in the teachers' room. The dingy maps were spread all over now, leaning against chairs and table legs; they'd been coming to class with Citizen Bola. Whenever he set one up against the blackboard he pointed out all the countries with new names. That hard to label, the world seemed false to Ruzi. She could not imagine Miss Christina in the vast pale splotch that was America.

Seated at the table, chin in hands, Miss was staring at Asia. When she turned, Ruzi said, "Miss, you made an error."

"Let me see."

Miss concentrated on the paper, teeth shut hard. "You cheated," she said finally.

Ruzi protested, although she had, in fact, copied the text from Mintu's book of fables. His school had used it his senior year and he'd said it might help. When Miss had told the class to write a fable, Ruzi had copied the one about Tarantula and Crocodile. Then she'd helped Mbonani, Nzuzi and Sanza by lending them the book. Helping was *good*.

Teachers didn't read homework. Ruzi was often returned papers with no marks but the grade at the top. Some teachers didn't even collect homework. So Ruzi had felt safe copying only the first two paragraphs from the text even though the fable went on four more pages. She figured she couldn't do worse if she wrote her own English.

But zero!

"I warned you," said the teacher. "If you cheat, you get zero." Ruzi remembered the word *warn* from a recent lesson. On the board Miss Christina had drawn a palm tree with all the fronds blown in one direction, squiggly lines for the wind, and then two people outside a hut with a thatch roof. The word *good-bye* hung in a bubble like a cloud over the boy, while the girl pointed at the fronds.

Miss had turned to ask who the girl was and everybody knew; she appeared regularly on the board with the new vocabulary words. "Lolo!" the class chorused. And who was the other? "Tuli," they shouted, "her friend!" Everyone clapped, the drawings with Tuli and Lolo together were best because they were getting married.

"One person," said Miss, holding up one finger so the class would not answer all at once. "What is Tuli doing?"

Sanza in the front raised her hand. "He is leaving."

Yes, he was saying good-bye. The class explained, student

by student, with last week's vocabulary, that Lolo was looking at the *wind* and that a *storm* was coming. "Don't go!" was what she said to Tuli.

Then Miss began to draw again. In the new picture Tuli was on the road by himself under a big cloud, a real one this time with a crooked line for lightning in it instead of words. Rain slanted down from the cloud; Tuli dripped.

"Is Tuli happy?" Miss asked. Palms drummed on desks: No! Intelligent? No! Was he surprised? (And there Miss shaped an "O" with her lips.) No. Why not? Because Lolo *warned* him.

They went around the class making sentences with the new word, *warn*. Ruzi had said, "I warn you about boys," and everyone had laughed, even Miss.

Now Miss was sober as she handed the failed composition back to Ruzi in the teachers' room. "I warned you," she repeated. Then, "I have the same book."

"No. Not cheating." Ruzi tried to look injured, but Miss told her to leave.

At the door, she saw the girls filing back into classrooms, a layer of white shirts above blue skirts sucked inside the building.

"Ruzi!" she heard.

Miss had learned her name.

Funny French replaced the slow English. "Ruzi, you don't need to cheat. Come for tutoring. Come in the afternoon."

She didn't have to, but she went, twice each week. First just to see, then she didn't know why. Other girls went, too; sometimes Ruzi had to wait, flipping the pages of her notebook, because Miss explained each person's problem alone. At the dining table Ruzi watched the blunt fingers write out sentences, lists and charts. Saying words was easier than writing them. Even in French, Ruzi had trouble putting her thoughts on paper. In her letters to Mintu, Bola never seemed to fit.

After lessons, Miss would show photographs of America, some very white with snow where people looked fat in thick clothes. She played tapes of American jazz, which sounded full of air. Ruzi scanned the room for foreign things, made Miss explain the battery recharger, the vitamins, the insect repellent which smelled so bad. Miss had no American perfume or cosmetics, she said. She didn't seem to like them.

Visitors were always knocking, if not students, then teachers whom Miss asked to come back later. "Come this evening, I have beer," she would say, "We'll play cards." A truck merchant brought her a case every few weeks, but instead of selling bottles she invited men to share. Twice at dawn, returning to the dorm from Bola's, Ruzi saw men leaving. One she knew from his antelope walk: the seventh-grade teacher. The other she was too far away to tell.

Wives never visited, but the children from next door came banging, buckets in hand, whenever their cistern was empty. Then Ruzi missed her family, imagined her own little sisters spilling water the way these kids did as they picked up the pails that Miss placed on the floor by the kitchen sink. Ruzi wanted little heads to braid.

When she was not at Miss Christina's or Bola's, Ruzi spent her free time braiding hair. Afternoons, the girls practiced on each other, grouped in pairs on straw mats under the mango tree. Ruzi braided best, twisting beads and colored thread inside loops that never fell. Relaxed in old rapas tied loosely so they could sit on their heels, they all told everything, what they knew and what they'd heard, whose lover was best. Ruzi talked about Mintu, meeting him at Abi when they were both visiting relatives; she'd been only twelve the first time, hadn't even worn lipstick! They'd been waiting so long to marry because of silly school; would her father make them wait until the full dowry was paid? Mintu wouldn't have money until he finished studying, for two whole years. Ruzi paraphrased his letters, the parts about how beautiful she was, and her friends laughed and sighed, but then they worried with her that he'd fall in love with someone else and marry against tradition.

By December Ruzi had filled three copybooks with English notes where her own delicate handwriting alternated with Miss Christina's scrawl. The teacher bit her lip as she wrote, crouching over the pen so her back arched unnaturally. Yet each time she lifted the pen and looked up, shoving the book towards

Ruzi, she smiled, pulling damp strands of hair away from her eyes. When Ruzi told her about Mintu she smiled, too, until Ruzi asked who *she* would marry. Miss said she wanted to work and travel, not marry, and when Ruzi kept asking questions the white face got pink the way it did in class when Miss was about to shout.

Ruzi never laughed, although in class everyone else would each time Miss stood turning color, the corners of her mouth wiggling like the tips of leaves in the smallest wind. Miss was funniest when she shouted. Once when Nzuzi stole her roll book she exploded, her English sentences strung together like the cars of a fast train.

At school she was angry more and more, slamming her books together before she left class even when the girls were trying to understand. But her lessons were strange; she rarely used the stories in the grammar book. Instead she brought dittoed texts about current events like overpopulation, or what to feed babies, or about wars in countries whose names Ruzi never remembered. All were written by Miss in English; Ruzi would hear the typewriter drumming as she arrived for tutoring, saying to herself new words like *ambush* or *lactate*. Lolo and Tuli were married with three children, but no longer liked each other. Miss had taught *divorce*.

In some ways, Miss Christina was like Mrs. Baxter. But instead of God, Miss talked about birth and death. Both women wanted to change Tambala. Miss wanted to so badly that when the girls couldn't learn, her own mind broke. When she said they should have few children, Tusamba told her she was wrong, that for parents children were money, and that Tambala was all empty space anyway. The rest of the class cheered, the hibiscus face perspired, everyone laughed, and Miss let out her ugly word.

Ruzi noticed that Miss used it often in its own paragraph, if that's what a paragraph meant, alone with lots of silence. In French films Ruzi had seen angry whites shouting words about the body or death, sometimes at no one. Tambalan had those words, but only for calm talking.

Miss needed quiet hands in her waterfall hair. Ruzi's knots, though, were meant for dense tufts close to the scalp; on Miss they wouldn't hold. Ruzi thought she could fix Miss's nails instead. Before the midyear vacation, the last time Ruzi went for tutoring, she promised to bring Miss some nail polish. She formed the English words, "Then you will be pretty. Then you will be happy."

Miss had put her hands under the table, in her lap. "I'm happy, Ruzi."

"No children. No husband."

Miss brought out her hands and lay them flat on the wood. The nails didn't grow beyond the skin at all, and a few fingers were scraped raw at the tips. White fingers looked weak, painful.

"Very small." Ruzi pointed at a nail.

"I bite them."

That puzzled Ruzi, even when Miss explained in French that it was a nervous habit. Quietly, she added, "I don't think Tambalans have nervous habits."

Ruzi's fingers were slender and competent. Braiding, they twisted back and forth, back and forth like village dancers to drums. Her shiny nails worked like a comb, her palms pressed the tufts flat.

Home for the holidays, she had found her mother dressed as usual in billows of pastel fabric. Sometimes it was silk from France. Mostly she was draped in cotton as she moved through the house, in and out of rooms, down halls, up stairs so gently Ruzi never heard her. As Ruzi was unpacking the day she arrived, her mother commanded, "Come and braid my hair."

Ruzi turned to see her heavy figure in the hall, bare toes visible beneath the curtain of her skirt. When Ruzi had first said hello she'd noticed the hair, knotted into rows with small shells woven in, curving in parallel lines from temples to spine.

"Can we keep the shells?"

"They're for you."

They sat in the courtyard where her sisters were cleaning

fish. Mbengi grinned, waiting her turn. "I'll be beautiful," she said.

The shells were tiny inward-curling things, with speckles of brown and red. You found them sometimes at the ocean; they were rare in Bossi. Mostly they remained from when they had been used for money in ancient times. They were like little tough-skinned flowers, Ruzi thought, unthreading them one by one from her mother's hair. Mbengi would wear them next, then Ruzi herself would wear them back to school.

"Lutete has spoken to your father," said Ruzi's mother.

Lutete was Mintu's father. That meant marriage plans. Ruzi's fingers felt like someone else's.

"For when?" she asked.

"When you finish school. Your father will accept a first gift and wait for the rest until Mintu can pay. Mintu is coming Friday to present the gift."

Ruzi was at the end of a complicated knot but she let go to hug her mother, then her sisters. "And I thought Papa was greedy!" She held the youngest by the shoulders. "You have a fine Papa," she said.

When Ruzi finished braiding the shells into Mbengi's hair the rows were uneven, the knots bumpy. "You weren't sitting still," she accused, and Mbengi answered, "Is this how you'll do your children?" But they were laughing.

Mintu arrived Friday in a taxi and lugged to the door a case of bottles. Instead of palm wine or beer, he brought American whiskey. Ruzi's father didn't drink much, but he nodded with excitement because he could sell bottles. Only as they sat for the conference did he stop shaking Mintu's hand. Then he waved everyone away, ordering Ruzi's mother to bring glasses. After a while Ruzi's brothers were invited to join them with two more glasses, and finally the women were admitted to the salon where the men were settled deep into cushions on the chairs. A ceremonial toast was poured, even a few drops for each younger girl, and when the congratulations were fading Ruzi asked Mintu to come outside.

"Why haven't you written me?" he asked as they found stools on the patio.

"What would happen if I didn't pass this year?"

"Are you failing?"

"I will unless you talk to my teacher. He'll leave me alone if he believes I'm getting married."

"What?"

"It's an arrangement," Ruzi said, deep and fast so it sounded hateful as crazy white words. She waited, and felt Mintu's hands around hers tense up. He was good. He'd be angry, but not at her.

Mintu whispered, "Were you doing so badly? Is that why you didn't write? You should have told me."

Ruzi tried to find stars, but the glare of the city filmed over the sky. Kundu had so many stars.

"I'm sorry," she said. "I didn't know what to do. If I failed, we would have had to wait longer. You might have stopped waiting."

"Do you like him?"

"He's a rat," she said, and started to cry. His arms went around her, the solid night arms she'd created out of Bola time after time.

"I'm going to Kundu tomorrow. He won't bother you again."

She wiped her nose on the hem of her rapa; she'd change it when she went inside. Mintu leaned away; she felt him trying to see her. Of him she saw only outlines: hair, nose, jaw. Hard, broad jaw.

Ruzi returned to school with the nail polish. When she asked Miss Christina the first day back if she could come that afternoon, Miss laughed, holding up her stubby nails, but said yes anyway. Miss laughed all through her lesson as students made sentences about Christmas and New Year's. Miss was happy. With blue chalk she drew water, where she'd gone. Copying down the word *ocean*, Ruzi wondered if Miss was happy to be back at Kundu, or to have left. Maybe she'd been with a man. Maybe she was getting married, too.

They sat outside on Ruzi's straw mat that she had brought rolled and balanced on one shoulder. No English books today; this visit was special. As they settled, Miss crosslegged and Ruzi sitting on ankles, Ruzi told the news. She punctuated her French with the percussion of tiny balls inside as she shook the bottle of polish. Like a calabash.

"Congratulations," Miss nodded, looking pleased as her nail turned red as a tomato. Her skin, too, was dabbed red at the tip.

"My fiancé studies agriculture, he's going to work for the state."

"And what will you do?"

"Children, Miss. And I can braid hair for extra money, while Mintu is in school."

Miss swallowed.

Ruzi started on the third nail. She wanted to ask about Miss's men, and began with, "You need a husband, Miss."

"You're wrong."

Ruzi tried to explain. Married, women mattered.

"Your English is so good now. Doesn't school matter?"

Ruzi's brush hovered over the pinkie. Now she was angry. If she were white, she thought, she'd be red as the polish. "I'll tell you about school. Girls go to school so bachelor teachers don't have to get married! We go to school so our dowries will be high, so our fathers will be rich. And since we can't marry until we finish, there's nothing to stop teachers like Bola!"

"Bola?"

Ruzi realized that Miss hadn't known. After smearing polish on the pinkie, she dropped the hand. What could this stranger understand about happiness? Miss was not intelligent enough to be a teacher.

Ruzi told her about the arrangement and Miss went hibiscus color, spitting out the ugly word.

Ruzi said, "Give me your other hand, I will finish."

However, Miss was unfolding, rising, slipping her feet into thongs.

48

"Miss, you can't leave, we've only done one hand. Come sit down, it won't take long." One hand of red nails and one of white was grotesque, like a cripple.

"If you were less worried about nails you wouldn't have this problem with Bola."

"But it's over, it's fixed!"

Miss Christina didn't hear, she'd already slammed her door. Ruzi thought of the hollow rattle of hinges that echoed at school each time Miss ran home, angry at everyone laughing, mid-lesson. They would crowd the classroom windows, listening. They wondered if she cried.

The next day everyone whispered about the five red nails; what did they mean? Muslims grew the nails on their little fingers long enough to curl like horns. Maybe in America people without churches painted their nails like Miss.

Ruzi didn't tell.

When Miss called on her, the pale eyes saw something se-cret, like when Miss had looked at Asia. Although Ruzi's an-swers were correct, Miss didn't smile. No smile, no red. A ghost face.

That afternoon was Tuesday, Ruzi's tutoring day, but when she knocked at Miss Christina's door no one answered. As Ruzi returned to the dormitory, avoiding mangos fallen from the trees, she saw Miss striding fast at the end of the avenue, skirt swishing. The principal lived over there.

Ruzi joined the girls braiding and offered the shells from her mother's hair. Tusamba wanted them, so Ruzi sat behind her, combing out the old braids. She told the story of Mintu's visit to Kundu. He'd spoken only to Bola. Mintu was tall with muscles tough from working outside; all he'd had to do was warn the little rat, and Bola had promised to give Ruzi "Bs" at the end of the year. That morning in the hall, Bola had actually congratu-lated her.

Ruzi was beginning to braid when Miss came thudding up the road.

She was redder than ever, "like the sun before it disappears," said Tusamba.

The road was sticky from the morning rain, and a thick layer of mud covered Miss's thongs. Only Ruzi knew why she was angry. Whites always got angry about sex. The principal had probably been polite, but he wouldn't care; he had his own way of helping. For money he would change student records.

When Miss Christina was alongside the girls, she stopped, mismatched hands on hips.

"Good evening, Miss," they chorused in English.

Her French came out like thunder. "Why are you girls always playing with hair? Every afternoon you're out here giggling like idiots, trying to make yourselves beautiful, and for what? So your men will think you're good enough to treat like animals!"

Tusamba straightened. "We're not animals."

"Then stop acting like them."

As Miss started towards her house, Ruzi could see the specks of mud on the backs of her legs. Whites didn't know how to walk slowly. Tambalan women knew to lift heels from mud carefully. Laughing with everyone else, Ruzi was sad. How sad that Miss had no friends, did not even want any. Men were all she had. No one to fix her hair or nails. What did white women talk about? Were they all so worried, reading and writing? Didn't they gossip, sing, touch? Miss's hand had felt cold, sick; Ruzi couldn't hold it again.

What They See

Zola wanted the clear kind. Not the dark green or brown ones hung on cardboard in market stalls. Not the kind the traders wore as they stood behind tables of wristwatches and belt buckles, nodding to the beat of radios like blind men. When the sun was a lemon up high, Zola could see himself in all those lenses puffed out like he'd eaten lots for days. He liked seeing himself fat that many times. Brown as a ground nut and fat. Really he was bony, old enough to be near man-size but hardly taller than the tables. His mother said as a baby he'd almost starved. Maybe all those bloated Zolas in the lenses had been eating his food. But he never wanted those dark glasses that hid eyes. He wanted to see.

People who wore the clear kind were smart. Almost all the whites did, and Africans only if they'd been to university or were old. Men in glasses wrinkled their foreheads and swung briefcases as they trotted to work; everything about them but their skin was white. The President had forbidden ties for men and pants for women, but Zola knew that if people were to really stop acting white those invisible glasses should be banned. With them you could understand science and medicine and live a long time. You could see very far, all the way to Europa, maybe to the afterworld.

He knew he'd never be rich, never wear a suit with short sleeves or leather shoes, never buy the French blue jeans in the store window, or even a belt buckle. His brother Mika might; he had the highest points in his class and was big. Zola would be happy if he could just see what they saw through those naked lenses. Colors must be different, everything would sparkle. What if buildings were like the bolts of cloth standing on end in the market—rows and rows of prints so different the flowers from one jumped into the trees of the next? And the piles of rubber thongs and plastic dishes—did they glow?

He had been waiting all week by the sugar. Madame always came to this Mama, and so he sat beside this lady trader so fat she hid her chair. Her arms were so wide she could barely lift them to measure out the cupfuls. The first few days Zola just sat, but then she started him wrapping small amounts of sugar in paper cones to lay on her table beside the sign: *50 makuta.* At the end of each day she gave him a full cone.

He knew Madame would come, strutting rich, ankles black as new car tires.

She went daily to buy fresh food; from the shade of a table spread with spices he'd crouched, watching. First, the shoes came clicking with hard heels in uneven steps as she straddled puddles of old fish water. Never the same pair, always the same click. If it were too crowded he might not see her head wrapped in cloth to match her long skirt, or her strong arms as big around as his legs. If so, Zola would wish to see through the table top above his head; with her glasses he bet he could. Through the legs hurrying past, or stopping, or bumping into someone stopped, some bare with thin hairs and some wrapped in skirts, some feet without shoes and some with heels, he had seen her across the aisle touching the tomatoes separated in clusters of three or four for 35 makuta, or the onions in beige skins sold one by one, or the beans—pails of beans speckled with red, yellow, or brown! Large, round ones or tiny long ones. What did she see through her glasses as she decided, shoes inching left and right and left again?

Sometimes she headed for the books, and then he would run down a parallel aisle, scurry across under display tables, and find a spot of shade to blend into. He could hear the quick shoes coming. When he saw the hips rolling towards him he thought of his mother, how she would look all wrapped in fancy cloth. With glasses he could probably see her dressed up even though she only had faded cloths and none for her hair.

As Madame moved closer, the hips would roll like a song in time to the clicking heels and stop across from him at the best book stall. It had to be the best because she always stopped there, picked a book and opened the cover, pink nails slipping beneath the pages, turning them, floating up to her wide nose to push back the glasses. She entered books through those glasses. Whenever a trader allowed Zola to hold a book, to go beyond the thick cover to the words within, nothing made sense. But with those glasses he would see!

Before he started coming to the market instead of school, he had learned to say the alphabet and write out words, but in books there were too many. After the teacher had called him a fool and the whole class laughed he never went back. That teacher wore glasses. Zola had asked for his old pair when he had come to school with huge black frames instead of the wires. The teacher laughed, and told him about a doctor. Although Zola had known glasses were special because he'd never seen them for sale in the market, only that dark kind everybody wore, he hadn't guessed their medicinal power. A doctor's magic was stronger than a fetisher's; in the village all *they* did for eyes was to put paste over the closed lids of people who had nightmares.

Glasses could make fire. Once the teacher took everyone outside when the sun was hottest, took off his glasses and lay them on a piece of paper. Under one lens on the clean white, Zola saw a brown spot turn black and then curl up in a flame. So he knew the teacher was keeping the old pair for their magic.

Mika did not agree. He saw into books with his own eyes, he said; his magic came from within. "You listen too much to those village tales. Didn't your teacher tell you about bending light? It's physics." But after speaking a long time over a page of odd squiggles and lines that looked to Zola like witch writing, Mika said, "Don't worry, it's not for you."

No one minded when Zola stopped school.

The sugar was the best place even though Madame didn't come there often. When she did, she bought a lot, and the Mama trader would fill a clear plastic bag by the cupful from the burlap sack sitting on the ground. When Madame bent down, counting the cups to make sure she wasn't cheated, her head was low enough for someone as short as Zola to reach those eyeglasses. He'd had to wait extra days wrapping sugar in paper cones while the Mama yawned and chewed kola nuts, but he was right. There she was.

Today the shoes were red, in a hurry as usual but never slipping on mud or spilled guts. And above the shoes came a curtain of bright fish swimming in pink seaweed rippling to the right, then to the left, as the knees moved forward. Clickety-click.

He wasn't under a table but right out there beside the Mama trader, folding paper in a spiral.

"Hello, Madame," Zola called, just like any trader boy so she would go to their table instead of someone else's. When she asked how much, he looked over to the Mama, who sighed, "500 makuta a kilo. Price still the same." Madame nodded, her glasses slipping down her nose, and the Mama gave Zola a plastic bag.

He didn't want her money, not even her earrings, the gold fish swimming through the air from her earlobes down towards her black shoulders. Just the glasses. She was rich, she could buy more. She was leaning over, counting as he scooped and poured the yellow grains right inside the clear plastic so not a speck was lost.

He dropped the bag with the cup still draining into it, snatched the glasses, and ran.

"Thief!"

He slowed, just for a second. No one had ever called him that. Thief men pulled earrings right through the lobes, left women bleeding and wailing. But he was bad now; with the glasses warm in his hand he kept running. Yes, the sugar had been a good place because the market ended there and he could run faster in the street. He had seen men caught, how they got hit again and again. Already the glasses were working; holding them he was running faster than ever, dodging all the cars and bicycles until he got to the river.

Zola's secret place was under the trees near where rich people lived in huge houses behind thick walls. He liked the space, he could look way over the water to the green strip on the other side. Boats were black dots. It smelled of machines and fish, but not as fishy as the market where flies jerked in circles around the pink slabs.

He was breathing harder than the Mama trader would when she lifted burlap sacks off her cart in the morning. Before he tried the glasses he blew on the lenses the way his teacher had, and wiped them on his shorts. Without fingerprints they were clear, the orange rims like candy.

But they were so large he had to hold them to his eyes; the sides stuck out behind his ears. He saw nothing. The green horizon was lost in grey; water became sky. The boats had drowned. Turning to the fluffy mango trees, Zola saw only monstrous green spirits—no branches, no leaves. Nothing moved or talked. The world curved away, as if his eyeballs had swollen up. He waved his hands; he'd lost his fingers.

In his pocket was the paper a beggar had given him. The man gave them to everyone because he couldn't talk; Zola wanted to read the words with glasses. And the letters were lost. He turned the paper over, upside-down. He would tell this man that people in glasses could not read his notes. Maybe they could only read science. If Zola wore them long enough, he would, too. He'd grow into them, they'd make him grow the way they'd made him run. His eyes felt so big. He would sit at the river every day where no one would see until he saw so much his head bulged out to fit the frames.

The Baobab

I wanted to step into Africa as if into a movie; suddenly everything would speed up, on the verge of happening. Drums would incite tribes. Or I'd bounce across the savannah in a Land Rover pursued by giraffes with those exaggerated necks. Instead, everything slowed down.

But if nothing happened to me during my two years at Sundi on the huge river, I did hear stories. Most had to do with Pili: stories either about him or that he told me. Sundi was Pili's maternal village, and by the time AfricEd sent me to that isolated bush post as a pioneer teacher for the new high school, Pili was already a legend, the local boy gone rich in Bashushi City, owner of the Golden Pot Restaurant and Dance Bar. Young for a legend, he was not yet thirty.

He visited me often at Sundi. When the wiry, tough-looking man fancy in creased Western dress first appeared at my door, I was already craving distraction. My first month or so had exposed Africa's great threat as boredom. I had, after all, no electricity. No old films on TV. Not even a cinema; no screens filled with inflated kisses. School finished at noon after beginning at the cool hour of seven, and the afternoons stretched endlessly. Children came to my door with pineapples;

women braided my hair. The novels that had lined one side of my suitcase were all read.

"I know many Americans," Pili had said, as if brandishing credentials, and then introduced himself with a long name I immediately forgot. "And you, I think, are Lydia?"

I nodded as we shook hands outside my mud house. His friendliness worked; his awe of America flattered me, and it seemed perfectly natural for him to say, "I invite you for a glass of palm wine, to tell me about your country."

We ambled down the dusty avenue, the heat buzzing, children chorusing, "Bye bye" from shaded perches, close to walls or trees. But they were screaming something else, too: "Pili pili pili pili." *Pili pili* was Zobolan hot sauce.

Waving back along with me, the stranger explained his name. As a child he'd been nicknamed Pili Pili because he was energetic, always into things. The name had stuck because he was in the restaurant business.

We stopped and sat at a table before Theodore's, the village palm wine bar that played scratchy Zobolan records over and over, tinkly salsa drumming back into itself.

"This is my place; my brother takes care when I'm gone," Pili said, and then I knew that this was the boy done good I'd heard about, Theo's brother.

Theo came out, lanky and slow, respectful, rubber thongs snapping. He furnished two glasses and an old whiskey bottle full of the milky palm wine, which he poured. After he went inside we heard the lurch of a needle on the battery-operated record player. A chorus whined. Speakers set facing out the windows crackled.

Pili spoke of the Golden Pot. "Good music up there." He winced at the blaring static. "I pay a deejay, he sits behind glass to play the records. You must come there, Lydia, be my guest and dance." And he began his story by pulling from his wallet photographs of his fine friend Gordon. In some of them Pili appeared, too, maybe ten years younger, in a school uniform.

One image sticks. All grin and muscle, Gordon towers over an impish Pili in mid-gesture. Gordon holds a soccer ball below his stubbly chin, head thrown back, short dark hair bristling. He wears fringed cut-offs. Beside him Pili flows toward the ball. His arm, caught by a slow shutter speed, blurs like smoke. A playing field stretches behind; in a second they'll spurt across.

Some Zobolans fear that photographs steal the soul. Is that what happened to Gordon? Who can explain what Africa took from him? Back in the States, he was never again the man in the photo.

I never met Gordon, but I feel I knew him. He was famous in AfricEd anyway, a case history cited at training lectures warning what not to do. Stay out of politics, was the rule. But even the director admired Gordon, I could tell, for bucking corruption.

"You may find yourself," the elderly Bixel had droned, swaying in his sandals, "in an impossible situation. Sometimes your work is impeded, you're wasting time. Keep"—he gave a little hop—"your integrity!" He concluded, though, that we should ask for a transfer. Unlike Gordon.

Pili had been Gordon's twelfth-grade student at Mbataki Mission, a few hours by truck from Sundi. And earlier on, he'd been a child cook for the missionaries, Doctor Twill and his wife, the original school principal. They had left before Gordon's time, still kept in touch, and were now helping Pili set up a visit to the States. Shouting over the music, Pili enunciated "the United States" slowly, licking and pursing his lips, broad cheekbones glowing.

I didn't believe then he'd go to America. My students all had the same plans. Everybody was going to own a car and a machine to wash clothes.

The next time I saw him in Bashushi City, he actually had gone, just for a few weeks, a sort of scouting trip to see if he might really set up an American business. We sat in the Golden Pot. The air-conditioned dining room was quietly clean with white linen tablecloths and sprigs of purple bougainvillea in clear vases. I was smiling, glad to be clean, three hundred kilometers away from Sundi village. The school's December break had finally swung around, and I was in the city to restock supplies and check in at AfricEd, to go out dancing and to movies.

Yet my visit with Pili in the Golden Pot was nothing like a date. I was an honored American guest; he had called his wife from the kitchen to introduce me. She'd bustled forward in a stained apron, smiling and bowing her turbaned head as we shook hands. Too busy to stay and talk, she quickly disappeared, leaving a charming impression of motherly sturdiness. Pili told me his two little girls were at home with an aunt. "And one day they will go to America. My wife will bring them for school."

Well, at that time I was romantically absorbed in an ambitious Sundi farmer, anyway. What Pili and I had in common was this fascination with each other's culture. To him, I imagine, I was simply a new addition to his collection of Americans who brought vital luck. Pili, however, as the villager with his foot in the West, was, to me, unique. As he was to everyone.

His visit to the States, he said, had been "too fine." From their home in California the Twills had arranged for mission people to meet Pili in New York. He had tagged along to a conference in Washington. He liked Washington. There, church friends offered to advise him in financing and other logistics. And it was Gordon's city.

During his few days in Washington, though, Pili couldn't reach Gordon. When he had found Gordon's telephone number listed and had dialed, he'd found the phone disconnected.

"I wanted Gordon to know he is sending me to America. Everything is from Gordon."

It was early, before the dinner crowd, which in Bashushi came late evening, European style. Two waiters in white pants and short-sleeved jackets hovered near the kitchen door, smoking. Pili wouldn't need them for a while; a liter bottle of Zobolan beer waited between us. "This beautiful restaurant, the waiters, the beer, all comes from Gordon." With his face framed by open hands pressing at each side, he told me about the gold.

When Gordon arrived at Mbataki, Pili was earning his school tuition by baking breakfast rolls for the students' refectory. The Twills had always paid his fees in exchange for his personal cooking, but they'd gone home after the president had nationalized all Zobolan institutions.

This shrewd leader discouraged tribal solidarity, and thus the internal tribal disputes which threatened his stability, by shuffling his officials region to region. Lugo, for instance, was sent to replace Mrs. Twill as school principal even though he was from the interior, his tribe a traditional enemy of the Bakongo coastal people. And Principal Lugo lived up to the stereotype of his tribe as crafty, bold, not to be trusted.

In the Golden Pot, Pili told wonderfully how he and Gordon had bumbled into Lugo one thick night. Since then, I've imagined the incident so many times, through Gordon's eyes as well as Pili's, that I tend to tell the story as if it were my own.

Pili and Gordon had gone to Sundi to find a football fetisher so Pili's class team could win. Gordon, as team advisor, had been asked to procure a charm. Football, or what we know as soccer, was about the only operating activity left by then at the school. Professors had quit teaching because Lugo never paid them. And Mbataki uniformly suspected Lugo of embezzling funds earmarked for teachers' salaries and the student food supply. Pili's flour had run out, and the students were going without breakfast.

Pili had engineered the trip and an alibi; he knew a football specialist near Sundi. Pili and Gordon could pretend to hunt bush rats the night they met the fetisher. The fetish objective was secret not only to guard Gordon's image as the Western scientific man but for practical magic reasons. If football opponents suspected Pili's team of using a fetish, they could contract their own fetisher for a counter curse in defense.

The night was wet. Not raining, but mucky and humid from the November dawn showers. Pili heard water everywhere and remembered the crocodile stories. Disguised, they rose out of water like men, came to shake your hand, then yawned back and bit, reptiles again. Pili led the way down the overgrown trail that paralleled the river. Brush grabbed at his shoulders and the forearms he raised to protect his face, and he pointed the flashlight down from above, beaming weeds and cracks in the path.

When the light swept right, over the black water, Gordon said, "No."

Gordon thought people might see the river flashing and find him tracking a fetish. Even more frightening was the dark path through rat territory; he wanted it constantly lit so he could see them coming. He hadn't heard the crocodile stories, at least not as a child, when anything is possible.

But Gordon's rat phobia made him glad he had a gun. This hunting rifle was merely the gracious loan of the Sundi Chief, who believed that Gordon's weekend visit was for tracking rats. Hiking at night was standard hunting procedure. The custom was to take a gun and flashlight, put out bait, and sit silently on haunches waiting for rustling. Then you stunned the animal with light in the eyes and shot.

"On the path!" Gordon urged, as Pili's light again swerved toward the river.

Pili admired Gordon for his courage in crocodile country while, behind, Gordon was cringing, mincing steps, imagining fur and claws streaking up inside a pant leg.

Suddenly Pili froze, a puddle of light flooding an eroded crack in the mud.

"What," said Gordon, moving his feet in place, afraid that stopping would encourage rat nibbles.

"You didn't see? In the water?"

Gordon had not paid attention to exactly what came up in the beam's sweep. But as they stood he heard a creak, a definite splash.

Pili jumped, shut off the light. "Crocodiles," he whispered.

"No, no. It's a boat, someone's docking. Who would cross the river up there? Is there a dock?"

Pili breathed slowly, loving Gordon. *Mundele* were immune to the ancestors from the afterworld below the river. He hoped. He'd never heard of a white person attacked. Gordon was his only weapon.

"Pili, what's wrong with you? Let's go. It's just people."

"No dock," was all Pili got out. When he still refused to move, Gordon groped for the flashlight and took the lead. He was sure he'd heard a nearby rustle, and didn't care to be sitting rat bait. Bush rats were a foot long, big as cats, "grasscutters," they were called. Like lawn mowers.

"No light!" hissed Pili the second Gordon flicked the switch, and he flicked it off. Meanwhile, scrapings, low murmurings, grunts and water slapping implied a cargo transfer.

"These could be crocodiles, not men," Pili whined, near tears. He had never wanted anything so much as to run. But then they'd go for him, away from *mundele* power.

Gordon pushed forward, not sure what was dangerous besides rats. He guessed the weeds' crackling was inaudible to the noisy crew ahead. The rifle pointed at a sky fuzzy without stars. The flashlight, in his other hand, pointed blankly up also. The rifle felt like a movie prop.

Then he became conscious of the rifle as rifle, how one might use it pointed level. He'd never had such thoughts, but here he was in a midnight jungle, his guide immobilized by fantastic crocodiles, and real people hurrying at something secret, close enough to be heard but not seen. Remembering the trigger, he decided his only problem was rats. Men he could handle.

He inched on, feeling with the toes of his snakeproof leather boots, until he was separated from the water noise only by a wall of weeds. He plunged through, crouching, nearing the voices carefully, not sure why except that's what Humphrey Bogart would do. The gun, Gordon realized, was making him stealthy.

At the edge of a clearing, a narrow strip of mucky bank, Gordon stopped. How could this be? That was Lugo, Principal Lugo, water to his knees. The huge girth was unmistakable. Even in the starless night his paunch glowed, puffing out a t-shirt. Now Gordon recognized the percussion of Lugo's short commands, and that the shadow quick to act was the school chauffeur. The third man was a stranger, had probably come from the other side with the raft.

Something sneaky was happening. Lugo had refused Gordon's request to borrow the school pickup. Lugo had said that he, himself, was travelling in the opposite direction to Tumpa, for school business.

The pickup could not be far. Gordon smelled again the inferno truck he and Pili had ridden out to Sundi, the rank blend of animals and oil. Chickens and goats had been crammed beneath the seats, and drums of oil and gas rattled in the back. Roofed with a tarp to keep the sun out, the truck had felt to Gordon like an open-air stew. He was sandwiched below the towering walls, between the sticky flesh of an old woman and Pili, who was dozing, jaw sagging. There was no air. Gordon was sure the rancid smell came from a suffocated animal. Bouncing, the bony woman was occasionally airborne and would jab Gordon in the leg as she fell. Gordon had nearly panicked by the end of the three-hour ride.

Panic waved over him again and settled as a great hate for Lugo, who had confiscated the very house meant for Gordon, the Twills' old house Pili had worked in. Gordon hated Lugo for riding, chauffeured, in the pickup from house to school, and for the way Lugo reached over the chauffeur to regally beep the horn before opening the door and touching his fat self down on Mbataki earth.

Gordon burst up, flashlight thumping to the mud so he could use both hands to aim the gun at Lugo's gut.

"*Mbote!*" he shouted, immediately regretting the word. This Zobolan greeting was what you said first when you saw someone; usually you shook hands after.

Big-bellied Lugo swivelled, facing Gordon. "Eh?" he peered. "What's this?" His tiny hands went up, back, and behind his shoulders. His belly stuck out further.

"Don't move," ordered Gordon. That sounded more like Bogart.

With a splash, the boat man disappeared into the river. He surfaced a moment later, swimming hard. Gordon wanted the raft. He wanted the pickup, too. He wanted any and all modes of transportation, he wanted never to ride another Zobolan lorry.

"Pili, it's O.K.! Hurry!" When he heard nothing, Gordon added, "The crocodiles are gone."

Pili emerged from the bush. Gordon got him to grab the raft, which was beginning to drift in the strong current. "Check the bags." They were piled, four or five of them, at the water's edge, beginning to sink in the mud. The chauffeur waited beside them, hands on his head.

Gordon couldn't resist. "What's in the *bag*, Lugo?" He drew out the word like a gangster.

Lugo blubbered. "For Mbataki, it's all for the school. My investment."

"*Shooah*, Lugo." Chicago style.

Pili gasped. "Gold, Gordon. It's gold."

Gold? Gordon felt his palms flush, swell around the gun. So this wasn't a game. Serious smuggling. Didn't smugglers have guns, too? Why wasn't Lugo armed? What was going on? Gordon's parody had turned into a bad dream. There was no sound track.

Lugo wasn't moving, he looked spooked. Maybe he was amateur. Maybe there was so much smuggling he didn't bother with guns, just paid people off. All Zobola was on the take.

Gordon thought. Lugo would have to run soon anyway, Mbataki had already mutinied. Lugo was probably planning to take this profit and disappear. Gordon could facilitate his exit.

Lugo and the chauffeur splashed onto the raft under Gordon's adrenalin-amplified voice. Eyes on the gun muzzle, Lugo didn't hesitate to tell where the truck was, just meters away. The chauffeur threw the keys on the pile of flour sacks. Pili pushed the raft with the paddle. The two were whisked by the current toward the river's center, and had soon dissipated into the fine line between river blackness and air.

In the Golden Pot, Pili sighed as I swished beer through my teeth, making foam.

"And then Gordon was gone," Pili continued, after ordering another bottle. "Just after. We hid the gold in the hole of a baobab near Mbataki."

AfricEd, as well as the Zobolan C.D.O., the president's secret police, went to see why Mbataki school was falling apart. Word had carried to Bashushi that the principal was gone, the school out of money, and that Gordon was a local hero. The president did not want any American local heroes disrupting his institutions, and AfricEd was embarrassed. So they sent Gordon home.

Pili brightened at the end of his story, purged of Gordon. "He always said, when he taught economics, that money makes money. Yes, especially in Zobola, money makes money."

Gazing side to side, up at the ceiling, marvelling at his enterprise, Pili laughed. "Gordon got his half out in dollars; on his way home he carried the gold to Bashushi and sold it, no questions asked. I never heard what he bought. I got some letters from Washington, and then none."

Pili didn't tell me then that his own money was making money through smuggling. Gold and also diamonds, in a big way. I didn't guess. It might have mattered then, when I was still fresh from America, where we make our own laws. But by the time I left I understood a world where survival justified parasitism. Understood, but didn't quite accept. Pili, too, had wanted out, any way possible; he wanted the luxury of being legal.

There's more. Veronica, Gordon, the Betterburger which became the Baobab Burger, Pili's American restaurant. Until he moved to the States the following August, Pili kept visiting Sundi, solidifying his gilded aura—the hope instilled in the village by his example. My own lover, an optimistic student taller, more dignified, and older than most, left his Sundi farm, and me, for Bashushi to get rich in Pili's wake. Sore and lonely as my second year began, I corresponded with Pili.

Now the usual roles were reversed: Pili had acquired the power of America, and I was a feeble villager. Of course AfricEd would have flown me home if I'd wished; now I see that I was playing a game, relishing the opportunity to act out poverty. Was it perverse curiosity that motivated me? I told myself I wanted to learn, but beyond that I had something at stake in

Pili's venture. I needed to see America through his eyes; I was testing my country. And then in a way he was my model, too. Just out of college, I still scorned the Puritan work ethic, the ideals of beauty and wealth. I knew I'd never be pretty.

So in Pili's letters I read of his first business, a Betterburger franchise in Fairfax, a suburb of D.C. Although his excitement was tinged with homesickness, he wanted to establish some stability in America before moving his family. The rare African man who found an opportunity to spend time abroad, for education or business or whatever, would not let temporary bachelorhood stop him; on the contrary, most would enjoy the freedom. And I sensed that Pili missed "fish *pili pili* stew warm on the table" and "clean clothes always ready" more than his wife.

I was surprised to hear after only a couple of months that along with a partner Pili was buying the Betterburger property and renovating the restaurant into "The Baobab Burger," with "more beautiful fast food." He'd met the partner through Gordon, which sounded safe, although Pili described Gordon as "different," "sad," and "angry." Letters always frustrate me with what's left out, but the mystery was too much when, around February, my mail from Pili stopped entirely.

Not until I was back in the States, my tour complete, did I hear what had happened. Pili told me in his new Baobab, Fairfax bright and hostile outside the window, June reflected in passing car metal.

I'd been in the country one week, at that point; everything was sharp and resilient. The pavement, the plastic. The wicker chairs were freshly manufactured, not worn smooth. I was flying to Los Angeles the next day, home to my worried parents. They would stand dumpy and trembling, I imagined, outside the flight arrival gate. My mother and I would cry. At home, she would follow me around with freshly baked cookies, begging for stories. I would be mute, I knew; my stories would clot. She would be proud and hurt. I would find a job and move out.

That's how I thought in Pili's Baobab Burger: not very far ahead. Pili's story took over, anyway. We sat with fruit juices at a wood table while, outside, muggy summer air amassed against the picture windows. Three girls in halter tops passed on the street; a truck honked. The wicker chairs left splinters in your arms if you tried to relax, but Pili said comfort was not important in a fast food environment. "Did you ever relax at a McDonald's?" he asked. He poked bone-colored straws from his glass of mangoade through his tight afro and forgot them, so they looked like skewed antlers.

In America, Gordon had withered. Rejected, rejected, was all he felt. Africa had been his refuge after a nasty divorce; he'd fled from his ex-wife, who haunted him with crazy phone calls. "You are going to die," she would whisper, and hang up. He recognized her voice. Pili said sadness, more than fear, had made Gordon move to Africa, far enough away, where the voice couldn't reach.

Then when he got evacuated, thrown out, Gordon's escape was foiled. He deteriorated back in the States, where nothing turned out. Pili couldn't understand.

"Why, Lydia?" he kept asking me. I can still see him, the tip of a potted palm curling over his head. Not quite a jungle. Yet he and his partner, Veronica, had done well: the place was a success.

Gordon was the catalyst between Pili and Veronica the first day he scuffed into Pili's Betterburger. Thin and hopeless, almost concave, he seemed more a sidling impostor with chapped lips than the Zobola Gordon of solid voice booming and hands fixing, full of knowledge and sacrifice. Pili had idolized him, hoping America would rub off, only to find now that Gordon hated fast food.

He seemed to hate everything, although he did rush forward, yelling, when he saw Pili. Gordon hadn't known Pili was in town until Pili had reached him by mail, after some research.

"Why Washington?" Gordon asked, after admiring Pili's good health.

Pili beamed, proud in his fresh dark blue jeans, ironed to creases down the front, with discreet flares where they met running shoes the color of brass. His shoes squeaked on the linoleum as he turned to slide into a seat. "I don't like New York. But you, how are you, my fine friend?"

Gordon was edgy, anger brimming out of pores. "This is not your kind of place," he said.

Did he mean America, or the restaurant? Pili hoped the restaurant. Gordon seemed to need help. Maybe he just needed food. He was sickly in his own rich country, skull-thin. Pili tried to see the smile Gordon had worn greeting him, but couldn't. This was a face not used to smiling. Pili had seen many in Washington, the avoiding, street eyes.

Gordon refused to eat at Pili's. In Zobola to refuse a host's offer of food was an insult, but this was America. Pili was confused. He was a fine manager, he knew; all his supplies were refrigerated behind the iron door, and his employees wore their hair in nets. His food came wrapped in paper and cellophane.

Gordon's objection began to make sense at Veronica's health food store. Gordon insisted they drive there in his old Datsun, so Pili could learn how to "eat healthy."

Veronica's was magic. Food was sold in its very essence, as powders and syrups, like medicine. Pili had seen vitamins before, all the *mundele* in Zobola took them, but here were grains, jellies, herbs. The store smelled sweet as a drug; you wanted to stop and rest.

Pili wandered the aisles reading labels: "Vitamorning Drink" was purple dust in an envelope; "Aciditrim" came in a box full of small jars, a different color for each day of the week.

He found Veronica fixing something from a shiny machine like his milkshake maker at Betterburger. "Vitamin B banana shake," said Gordon, who balanced on a tall stool, a leg out at each side. "Want one?"

Pili nodded, climbing up beside Gordon. The woman was full of vital force, Pili could tell, although all he saw from the back was a long mane like lemonade. Betterburger rules required all hair in nets, but this hair would add energy to any drink.

When she turned and looked at Pili her eyes reminded him of diamonds, not dull and dirty like the Zobolan ones he passed across the border, but like the diamonds cut, set in gold, and displayed under glass here in the States. Her eyes were mazes of light. She kept looking until Gordon said, "Same for him."

They spent the afternoon talking of nutrition and Buddhism, Veronica rising from one of the high stools whenever a customer entered. She had no employees, she said; business was slow. Health food was no longer exotic. Pili could tell she wasn't making money.

Gordon was withdrawn. He got up to go, sat down. He did this a few times. But each time he moved, Pili would turn from Veronica and say, "But you haven't told me. . ." and ask about Gordon's house, his job, his friends. Pili learned that Gordon had lived alone in his place way downtown for five years, had no job, had never gone back to school, never travelled. Pili was stunned. This was an inverse Gordon, *mundele* energy extinguished.

Pili asked why; Gordon answered, "I don't have to," and slurped at the final froth of his second vitashake.

He needed more, Pili thought. Maybe he couldn't afford to eat; America was expensive. These shakes, however, cost twice what Pili had offered at Betterburger. "So how do you live, with no job, no wife?" Pili asked, while Veronica was away at the cash register. "And the gold money, you lost that?"

"Money doesn't last long here, Pili. But it got me into business, something like what you do in Zobola."

"Diamonds? Gold?"

"Drugs. Nothing too risky."

Nothing too profitable, either, Pili thought. Gordon's clothes were dirty and wrinkled, his long hair stuck inside a dingy collar. He wasn't serious. Pili compared him to all the suited men in belts and ties, with clean fingernails and teeth, who slid in and out of Betterburger. Smiling or not, they were serious, always getting back to somewhere. Pili liked that pace, he liked the high-tech jets he imagined in his own running shoes as he sped around. He looked down at them now; the laces were indeed tied. Even the laces thrilled him, spongy nylon so different from fibrous hemp.

Pili considered Gordon's logic. Did he deal drugs because he didn't have to?

The Baobab Burger was Pili's idea, although Veronica had started him thinking. "Innovate!" she commanded, hands on hips as she stood in the middle of his Betterburger. She was always there, angling her chin toward corners, commenting. She made him see. "We could really take off, you know. Africanize the old burger thing, add panache. People want a new hamburger."

And he'd thought of the baobab, squat fat-trunked tree of his homeland, vital to birds, lizards, insects, rodents. Each tree an ecosystem. From a television special he'd learned baobab ecology, but from Zobola he remembered the huge shade percolating with tiny noises: warbles, snaps, the fizz of leaves stirring. Americans needed the baobab, he'd decided; already it was on T.V. "Ecosystem" even sounded like something in Veronica's health food store. Her clientele would join his for a fast food burger full of life.

Was I jealous when Pili let drop that they were lovers? Although they didn't love each other too much. They were like magnets. Skin to skin, they were good. I'm guessing about this; all Pili said was, "She likes black men." They were tight until what Gordon did. Which happened the night of the Baobab's opening, in February.

I shifted in my chair, picked splinters out of my elbows and tried to picture Fairfax in winter, under snow.

Certainly I envied Veronica's looks. Now and then she swished through the kitchen door, saw us and stopped, hands on hips, as if she had forgotten what she was doing. I couldn't tell what she was thinking. Her crystal gaze was locked into a businesslike smile that bent the corners of her mouth up, out of shape. I don't know whether she was distant because of Gordon, whom she'd never liked, or just distant.

To Pili she was just a fly he whisked away with the licorice back of his hand when she focused enough to offer to refill our glasses. The dregs of my mangoade had crusted. I thanked her, sorry. Unconcerned, unapologetic, she didn't seem to hear. Pili

and she had already closed their deal; she was buying the Baobab. He would soon be in Zobola.

All winter they'd planned, Veronica outlining the market,
the local taste for the international, the vast pool of young
Washington professionals who were rich and guilty. Africa was
a hot topic since the famine. Africans had been starving a long
time, but suddenly everyone was talking about Ethiopia. Veronica's theory was that to Americans, Ethiopia was fun to pronounce; if you could say it, you were smart.

Thus she immediately bit Pili's idea for the Baobab Burger.
People would come just to learn the pronunciation. I had to
smile; I shared Veronica's cynicism. Yet her drive to cash in on
hypocrisy appalled me.

At the top of the one-page menu was the key: *bowbob*, beside a sketch of the tree. That was enough information, Pili had
said, for a fast food place. People didn't want "to be complicated."

While Veronica sold her health food store, Pili dropped his
Betterburger contract. They renovated. They advertised in holistic and culture ragsheets, they put up handbills. The public was
invited to opening night; all prices were halved.

Veronica's crowd came draped in Indian print shirts, fishermen's sweaters, and natural-color leather workboots that laced
above the ankle. They moved slowly, oddly anchored by the
massive down coats that hid their chins. Nobody smoked.

The dining area, still glassed on three sides, was divided into
smoking and nonsmoking sections, and the guests split conspicuously, all the holistic people together. Opposite were the people
who wanted a fast burger and ashtray. The smokers were the
more heterogeneous, from the quick people in suits to high
school kids looking for computer games.

The non-holistic people ate happily, hungrily. The health
people tended to eat with less energy, leaving half-moons of
their whole wheat buns and soy burgers on their beige paper
plates.

The evening was getting under way; the two Senegalese
conga drummers Pili had recruited from the Africa Center

downtown began to play. People tapped their bone-colored straws on the tables.

Pili had invited Gordon, along with any friends. Not until Pili was taking the mike from the drummers in order to welcome his guests did he see Gordon outside, a phantom suspended before the passing headlights of cars. Pili saw Gordon's palms pressed against the glass like the undersides of huge tropical slugs. The hands inched sideways, two slugs in tandem, lit white from the restaurant candles. Pili watched the hands as he spoke to the full dining room, as the conga drummers sustained a polite counterpoint.

"In Zobola we have a tradition," he began. "The host of a party must always speak and explain the importance of the celebration, so that all the people can come together in one happiness."

To Pili's left, on the front glass wall, the hands were pressed. Behind them the shadow was Gordon's; Pili recognized the down jacket flaring out at the sides because the zipper was broken. He recognized the dark balloon above as Gordon's tilted head.

Pili had actually bought Gordon a new red jacket after the first snow in November, but Gordon didn't want it. Oblivious to the protests, Pili had shoved the coat through Gordon's car window. After pulling out of his Betterburger parking spot, Gordon had hesitated at the exit, then pulled suddenly away so the jacket, pushed back through the window, had fluttered above the ground, arms spread.

Pili had not understood. Gordon's words echoed: "I don't have to." But what if you could, when before you couldn't?

The figure wavered, seemingly grounded by the suction of palms against glass. Pili wondered if his words were audible outside. "Everybody is welcome!" he shouted, and people exchanged glances.

"I want all the people from the outside, inside, I want those who are cold to become warm, those who are sad to be happy, we must eat together, share our troubles, rejoice in the vital force of these special organic foods here that will give us all long life!"

"Hear, hear," someone shouted, and a smattering of applause allowed Pili to remember his promise to Veronica.

"And while we are here getting strong, we can remember too the people with no food in Ethiopia, and leave at the counter, instead of a tip, coins for Africa." That was all, he didn't want to discourage appetites.

He looked up from the audience to see the hands ten feet across the glass, trailing a long smudge. They had moved past the front glass door without dropping to pull and enter.

Pili thanked the guests and called Veronica to the mike. The holistic guests cheered. Infected, the conga drummers beat down hard. Pili stepped around toward the kitchen, his way to the front blocked by a seated family—a short-haired woman, an exhausted man, and two boys who looked as if they were missing something on television.

Gordon was gone by the time Pili met the blast of freezing air. The cold was awful. In front of the Baobab, he studied the streaks cutting across the heads glowing in candlelight, Pili's little American crowd. He saw again the hands, but from this side, the backs chapped, tips of nails black, no rings. He saw the hands, disembodied, wiping.

Gordon's car was not in the parking lot, although many like it were, dull compacts with bent fenders.

Pili telephoned but the phone had been disconnected. He told me, his voice teetering, not quite cracking, "There was a great pain floating somewhere."

Listening in the Baobab, it seemed to me that the great pain, still connected to Gordon's tuberous hands, had now seeped inside the glass walls.

That night, Pili had left his restaurant opening, aware that Veronica didn't need him.

His car was dull and bent, too; he'd bought it second-hand after the end of his first and last quarter with Betterburger. The car always started, but the heater didn't always work. Pili bundled into the red discarded jacket, big enough to fit over his own. He kept it in the car for winter driving.

The police were at Gordon's apartment building, but Pili had already felt the gun go off in his head, in his heart, a deep puncture as he sped down the beltway. He'd felt a huge sudden silence, a suspension, a nothing. He knew death, Africans know death. Yet in America it was different.

In Africa, disease or accident takes life, the ancestors work behind the scenes. This was Gordon pulling his own trigger, the Gordon who hadn't wanted to hunt. This pistol had been registered several years in his name. The police had found evidence of drugs. They doubted he ever made any big, important deals. So did Pili.

Pili never warmed up, even after the slush melted.

"This is not right," he said to me, pulling a straw from his scalp. "This place is too much life." He meant the country, not the restaurant. "So much life people kill themselves, they don't wait for disease. Killing, killing. People die from craziness here."

"I know," I said. I couldn't stand it. I reached over and pulled the other antler out of his hair.

Pili is gone. In California I got a letter on Golden Pot Hotel stationery; he's doing well.

He couldn't make sense of Gordon; I couldn't help, although I know how Gordon felt at that opening, regretting his own spent gold, resenting Veronica: heir to white American opportunity, grabbing a chance by the horns to wrestle a profit. Perhaps she had once been devoted to the karma of alfalfa sprouts and communes, but finally money called, and she had the necessary gifts: personality, energy.

I don't have those gifts. And Gordon's gifts were buried in Zobola with his hero status and authority, his stardom indigenous to that land. My own Africa was sedate and undramatic, the sort AfricEd encouraged. I fulfilled my contract passively waiting for adventure, feeding on legends.

Blue Taxis

Kwame taught me tennis that summer. I was fifteen, back from boarding school, back with my father in Accra. He'd moved from our old house into one with a tennis court, next door to the Ambassador's residence. Every morning at six-thirty the Ambassador claimed the court, and usually I recognized his opponent as one of my father's colleagues at the Embassy. Looking up from my tea, I could see the game in fragments through the window: an arm and racket slicing past, a fair head suspended in a pose of concentration. Sometimes Kwame arrived early for my lesson, though, to rally a few minutes with the Ambassador, and I would hurry out to watch. Kwame was a pro, and he was an African, and he ruled the court with close to motionless efficiency. When he had to move he glided, flipping from forehand to backhand; when he hit the ball the sound reached into your chest. Opposite Kwame, Ambassador Whittier would scramble and lunge, kicking up the clay dust, smudging the white baseline.

My father didn't play. The fancy house was not his choice, and my mother wasn't there to take a stand. In Washington she'd been in and out of hospitals; I was ten when she died. After that, my father was transferred to

Accra. For two years we were at home in the American compound downtown, and he would have preferred, I think, to stay put. But he moved as a favor to an incoming boss who for some reason disliked the tennis estate. To my father, a house was a house whether palatial or modest; his trouble was in packing and dragging our home across town. Yet he made the swap, and people praised our luck.

It was Ambassador Whittier who arranged my tennis lessons, maybe because he felt that someone in the house ought to use the court. In any case, he took responsibility for his American community; he wanted us all busy and happy. I liked him. The summer before, he'd arranged a weekend trip up-country for the kids, sending us off in an air-conditioned van which he met at the border of Upper Volta—the nation now known as Burkina Faso—where he made no secret of changing money on the black market. Tall and cool, he had stood in front of the customs bungalow, counting greenbacks into the palm of an African in khaki.

My friends from the American school, where I'd spent seventh and eighth grades, had all left; most families did after two years, but my father had extended his contract. Since there was no expatriate high school, kids my age came only for vacations, if at all; some saw their families in the States.

This summer brought Cathy, another Embassy daughter; Whittier drove us both in his own cramped compact to meet Kwame at the Accra Tennis Club. "You'll like him," he said, passing a blue taxi. "He's very good, very sharp."

Cathy glared at her knees. Clearly Whittier hoped Cathy and I would keep each other company; I'd hoped so, too, and was disappointed. Her braid lay rigid as a brace along her spine, and she kept her pretty face averted, showing little more than a wooden profile.

I asked her how Accra compared to Bangkok, her father's last post.

"It's so primitive here!"

"And Bangkok's not?" I'd never been in Asia; I really wanted to know.

With an exasperated sigh she turned to the window. Her lack of pretense in the Ambassador's hearing amazed me; she might have won my admiration if she weren't snubbing Africa.

"The Thai are gentle and very intelligent," she said. "These people just charge around yelling, they come right up and put their sticky hands on you. They're always touching my hair. And they smell."

"Oh, you'll get used to that." The Ambassador winked in the rear view mirror. "Every country has its own smell, you know. Even ours. We all reek of disinfectant."

I laughed; Cathy kept scowling.

The tennis club had a colonial flavor, overstaffed with Africans in starched drill, resounding with good-sport voices, brisk with damp, thick-legged men. Inside, heavy pieces of furniture and an array of trophies cluttered a dim lounge; a bar spanned one wall.

I was blinking, adjusting to the dark, when a figure approached from the shadows. Kwame, smiling brightly in his tennis whites, stepped right up, shaking hands with the Ambassador. And I was startled by how small my hand felt in Kwame's; he was not built large. Twenty at the most, probably born back when Kwame Nkrumah was a hero, he struck me as vaguely incomplete.

"I am happy to meet you," he said, tilting back his head. Listening to Whittier, though, Kwame looked mostly down as he nodded, hands loose at his sides. Answering questions, he'd glance up and lean slightly forward. Again I saw the Ambassador handling money, although this time instead of counting it, he held out an envelope to Kwame, and I didn't see whether it contained dollars or the Ghana cedis. The fee had been arranged at the office with our fathers.

"Two half-hour lessons Monday through Friday, individual instruction, right?"

"Yes, sir." Kwame barely pronounced "sir," so that it sounded like an oddly emphasized "s." "Separate lessons are best to begin. Maybe later they will play together."

"Fine, that's fine. That O.K. with you, girls?"

"Sure," I said, unable to catch Cathy's eye. She nodded as if at someone across the room.

We agreed to meet Monday at my house. Saying good-bye, Kwame raised his hand so it flopped toward his forehead in a strange gesture—half salute, half dismissal, like a reflex he wanted to hide. Like most Ghanaian men, he must have trained for the army.

Cathy and I lagged behind Whittier in the parking lot. "What do you think?" I asked.

She shrugged. "About what?"

"Kwame. The lessons. Think he's good-looking?"

Here she flashed me a pale glance. Something in my face made her frown. "I just hope he's a good teacher."

Good-looking wasn't the word; none of the words I used for boys fit Kwame. Not "attractive," certainly not "cute." At our first lesson, the early light revealed his mixed blood—his skin the color of toffee, the unique smatter of black freckles spanning the bridge of his nose. Gazing down at me, chin tipped up, he held his weight in his heels, and seemed tall.

With his own racket, he demonstrated the grip and swing. Positioning my elbow, he smelled of soap and red pepper. His own stroke he fueled with beautiful restraint, his technique honed to instinct. Yet as I watched, I couldn't help thinking of that awkward salute.

Cathy was late; I decided to bring some water, although Kwame hadn't worked up a sweat. When I returned from the kitchen, ice rattling gently in the glass, he was standing calm and proper where I'd left him, inside the fence.

"Come and sit in the shade," I called.

He walked over, thanking me for the drink, and stared a second into it the way a white person would after spotting an insect. Then, turning slightly, he dipped his long fingers into the water and fished out the ice, tossing the cubes onto the lawn. In one draught, he downed what was left, then handed back the dripping glass.

"You don't like ice?"

"Eh, no."

"It's too cold?"

Cathy came trotting up, shouting, "Hi," as she headed for the net, and Kwame hurried after, wiping his hands on his polo shirt.

From then on, I brought his water chilled from the refrigerator. He never said much, and he saved his smile for the court, for my best hits. Day after day, he showed me where to put my feet, how to angle the racket, when to lean, how to get good contact and follow through. He stood in front of me dropping the ball for weeks.

One afternoon, I arrived home to find my father standing in the drive, clinking the coins in his pockets.

"I have to ask you not to go inside," he said. "Could you go around back, and wait by the court?"

"What's going on?"

"I can't say. Go ahead in back, and I'll join you in a minute."

He was wearing sunglasses, but even without them his grey eyes could leave me guessing. Not that he lied; he refused to explain because he was honest, and his quiet look was his way of earning my trust. I had always respected his secrets.

He turned his head as an Embassy car barreled up, crunching gravel. Flanking the black hood were two toy-like American flags. I started walking, looking back, and I saw three strangers with briefcases hurry past my father through the front door. In their white shirts and polished blunt shoes they looked like U.S. government, but I'd never met them.

I waited under the jasmine tree, on the same bench where I'd sit watching Kwame. Just then the gardener was pushing a heavy roller back and forth over the court, smoothing the clay. The rusty contraption had no motor, and the roller, about three feet in diameter and several in length, was solid iron. Glossy with sweat, he kept a steady pace, his calves hard as bottles, his bare feet pressing down. When I waved hello he smiled, but then he didn't meet my eyes again. Straining, he frowned, the tribal scars above his temples tightening like bolts. I looked away, conscious of being idle, but after he turned I stared at his crooked effort.

My father came quickly across the lawn, his light stride shot with tension. In his jacket and tie he looked lost as he hesitated under the tree, pulling out a handkerchief to wipe his brow and mouth.

"It'll be a few minutes."

I nodded. Things were too askew to talk. Here was my father dressed for work, perched beside me where I usually set my racket press and can of balls. Shut out of his home, he had no choice. We might have been two bad children.

Finally he cleared his throat. "They're looking for listening devices. They think the house is bugged."

He said he couldn't explain, and I thought I understood. I didn't think then of the shadow cast on him, that he might be suspected of leaking information—or that he might actually have done so. Of course, I never asked him if they found the bugs.

Checking his watch, my father stood. He went away and by the time he came back the gardener had finished with the roller and was repainting the white lines, inching backward in a crouch, bent above the red earth like a fist.

My father was still seeing Rochelle. She'd been bustling around him since Christmas, and I blamed her for my curfew. That vacation, a lively group of expatriate kids had formed, and since some were old enough to drive we'd ramble off to downtown movies, then hit the dancing clubs for Star, the good Ghanaian beer. Around one, we'd all be headed home. Until, that is, my father announced a curfew of eleven o'clock. It was Rochelle's idea.

With meddlesome cheerfulness she'd scuttle across a room, large pumps pointing outwards, straighten a painting or dim a lamp, and then pose before her handiwork, fingers hooked around her boxlike hips. She hummed, she smiled, she raised the two tidy loops of her eyebrows. When she zeroed in on me, I'd want to run, afraid she meant to poke at my posture or tug my hair. Actually, she touched me only once, near the end of the

82

summer, when I was due soon back at school and my father's tour was almost up. We'd had guests for dinner, and she must have been somewhat drunk, because she cornered me alone and clasped me in a hug. Startled and embarrassed, I didn't struggle, just let her bony arms cling; she held on tightly for a long time, desperate as a child squeezing a cat. When she let go I walked away.

Otherwise, she kept her distance, so that whatever she said or did to change my father happened behind my back. Out of the blue, he'd come knocking on my door to explain, politely, that I'd spent too much money on clothes the past year, or that I'd left the living room a mess. Really, his only unreasonable comment was about the curfew. "Fifteen is still too young for such late nights," he'd recited. He refused to tell me why, I thought, because he didn't know; I'd become his blind sacrifice to Rochelle's prim morality. More likely, he was simply too shy—a form of macho—to admit that he worried. Not about the drinking—he always poured me wine at dinner—and not about the hour; eighth-grade parties had lasted after midnight. It was the roaming loose in the streets, some kid at the wheel, and it was where I might be led, just old enough for independence to mean trouble.

At the time, though, the unfamiliar discipline felt unfair. Not long after the search of my house, hoping for an ally, I dialed Cathy's number, but balked when her hollow voice reminded me that we were not friends. We never talked after lessons; why now? The line crackled; lamely, I hung up. After all, likely as not, the phone was tapped.

I'm sure my father never pictured the sort of trouble I did get into; nobody would have—except, maybe, Cathy.

Since seventh grade, I'd gone faithfully to the Friday movies shown on the roof of the Embassy annex building—second-rate spy or cowboy flicks, or busty Italian comedies, junk no one really wanted to see, but all the kids would go. The school crowd filled the last rows, girls and boys holding hands, carefully entwined, sometimes kissing. The projectionist, named Experience, sat right behind and played along. "I be stealing your wife," he'd tease.

My old house had been a block from the annex, so I would walk at twilight to the films, and find rides home. Since the new house was across town, though, I learned to rely on taxis, pumping my arm as I saw the Ghanaians do to hail one. Our street teemed with the little blue Cortinas. Often a passenger or two stared from inside as I told my destination, and if the driver didn't grunt and drive off, we haggled for a good fare. I knew to check the tires, and the driver's breath for alcohol, before getting in, although I took for granted the holes rusting through the floor where you could see the road below blur, and the rickety doors that only the driver's magic touch could coax open and shut. Wedged between Western-suited men and gold-bangled matrons abloom in batik, I leaned into the curves. I loved the hint of palm oil under perfume, the smoke slinking out the window.

Sometime after the debugging, I went to the Friday film and sat up front with the adults. It felt like church, everyone beaming good will through generic questions like, "How is your father?" or, "What are you up to this summer?"

I was surrounded mostly by women abandoned by their kids in back, women frumpy and dazed as pioneers. I tried to imagine Rochelle dressed in their thick-strapped sandals and faded shifts, but her U.N. job kept her trim and sharp.

Apparently everyone but bored kids and their indulgent mothers had passed up tonight's spaghetti Western. Not even Cathy had come. As the projector squeaked alive, I slunk down in my chair, and the picture unfolded. Ragged gunmen stormed an adobe village where a señorita lay tied in a belfry.

At intermission I walked behind the projector to the far wall, and looked down into the street. Many times I'd watched the sleepy blink of cookfires and neon below, alert to roosters and car horns. Now I saw the neighborhood seething with camaraderie, knots of beery people sliding past each other, laughing and whooping, calling out in Fanti. I spotted, down the road, the glowing script that spelled *Nero's*, the club my

Christmas clique had liked best, and I listened for the bass strains of dance music, but it was too early; the Lebanese dinner tapes would still be softly pumping. Nobody would be there, not now, not later—at least nobody I knew. But if someone did invite me out, what then? My curfew would force me to lie, to sneak out. Beginning to imagine the scenario, some new acquaintance parked outside—but who?—I heard footsteps.

Cathy had arrived after all, and her jagged silhouette was jostling straight for me. "Cathy?"

"What are you doing over here?" she complained.

"Smoking."

I could hear her sniffing. "No, you're not. Look, my father's here, we came in late. Do you need a ride home?"

It sounded like his idea. "Thanks," I agreed anyway. "I was going to take a taxi."

"God, what a corny movie. Is that all they can get here?"

"We don't have to come. There must be something better to do."

"They don't even have T.V."

She was leaning over the ledge, looking all around. I thought of pointing out *Nero's*, but then she said, "Look at this place. Look at how our noble white influence lives on."

I tried to deflect her sarcasm. "England's, you mean."

"I guess there's a difference."

Scanning the familiar scene, I wondered what she saw. "And Thailand's held up better?"

"Thailand," she informed me, "was never colonized."

Peeved, I changed the subject. "How are your lessons?"

"I'm quitting," she said, then snapped back upright as if to address the town. "I'm tired of swinging at balls because Kwame's too lazy to rally. At first he said we'd do that for two weeks; it's been almost four. He's such a cheat."

Kwame? True, he had yet to work up a sweat, but then my swing was far from perfect. Or was it? But I didn't care, I wasn't any more eager than he to go loping around the court. "I'm such a zombie in the morning I never noticed. Maybe if we both say something."

"I already told him, last week. He just laughed, bouncing that dumb ball. He gives me the creeps."

I tried not to smile. Clearly, she'd failed to tap his charm. Of course, he never said much, but his grin had grown automatic. When I missed the ball we'd both laugh, just as we did when he fumbled one tossed by the ball boy.

She pattered off toward the floodlit chairs, and I turned back to *Nero's*. The lights behind me dimmed and the street below gained definition, potholes and bits of trash coming up. Alongside the cracked pavement, pedestrians had worn the dirt smooth, and I longed to feel that soft path under my bare toes. The sound track boomed with gruff bickering, exaggerated rustling, a squeal and cloth ripping; could they hear this in the street? I was embarrassed for my culture, for tainting the neighborhood with such barbaric noise. I did not envy Cathy's seat beside her father.

During a lull, a refrain from Ike and Tina Turner filtered up to me through *Nero's* open door as a group stepped outside; the door strangled the tune as it shut behind them. They were three young Ghanaians. I froze, squinting at the lithe figure in the middle, his gait fluid and understated between the swagger of his gesticulating friends. Kwame? My throat went dry.

They veered into the road. No—the man was too dark, too delicate in build, too meek. It wasn't Kwame, but it might have been his brother; both men walked with a lilt, chin high, loose in the shoulders and hands. Relieved, I felt silly. Why should the sight of him make me nervous? We could share a beer at *Nero's*, we could dance. Dancing, he would rock side to side, knees bent, fingers snapping as they did at ball boys on the court.

Opposite the annex, where the long American cars sat like docked boats, the men suddenly looked up. Thundering hoofs and an accelerated orchestra blared. The tallest raised a spindly arm, his small face puckered around eyeglasses, and like a fool, I waved. He had simply been pointing. As if my gesture cast a spell, they stiffened like statues at the same time the movie went quiet. Then the man swung his arm again, fist clenched, yelling. He stepped forward, glasses glinting, and I didn't get the words, but his skating voice made it clear that things were wrong and I was to blame. Right away, his friends yanked him back and on down the road until, as a single outline, they lurched around a corner.

They were drunk. Like a black net, the sky seemed to sag, clogged with stars. Once I'd wished on a falling one that I could stay for good. Once I'd walked the block as if it were mine, smiling at the kids always calling, "Bye bye!" What had happened to that time?

My old house was invisible from the annex roof. I turned to see the movie screen bristling with saguaro, mesas drifting left to right. Posted beside his projector, Experience sat hunched forward, head bobbing as if to some beat, although all I heard was a cacophony of hoofs. As I came up behind him, however, I saw that he was keeping time with the squeaking reel.

I touched his shoulder, and he jerked back. Then he recognized me. "It's you."

We'd already slapped palms hello that evening, friends from way back. I used to buy him Cokes.

I asked, "Do you know Cathy?"

He shook his head at his khaki knees.

"Cathy. A girl my age, maybe a little bit taller, skinny one, long brown hair all down her back?"

His eyes shifted thoughtfully. "That one all the time angry?"

"Yes. Can you tell her something for me? I'm going home now, catching a taxi home. Her father was going to take me."

"You be sick?"

"No, no. This film is bad."

We looked together at the movie, at the men draped slovenly around a campfire.

"It's a good film," he said. "The girl will marry that man."

"He's no good. He shoots everybody. Anyway, can you tell Cathy? She'll be looking for me."

"Sure thing."

"Thanks. I owe you a Coke." We shook hands hard, as if sealing a pact.

In the road I hurried past Cathy's station wagon, past where the man had thrust his fist in the air. The ground was not the pillow I'd imagined but packed dense, pitted and scattered with rubble. Hadn't I noticed often enough, sharing taxis, the callouses on people's feet?

Outside *Nero's* I heard the bass pounding. The song didn't matter now, nor the beer, nor even the sweaty, sexy dancing; if that's what I'd wanted, I could have gone straight inside. What I missed, I guess, was that bunch of us together trying to grow up, treading territory that was adult as well as African.

The concrete walls that led down the side street to my old house shone pink in spots, near the gates where nightwatchmen had their fires. I kept to the middle, avoiding each guard huddled in robes, until I saw Abdul. He sat perched neatly as ever on his little rug beside his fire, dozing.

Moving against the shadowy wall opposite, I inched forward until I could see, on the second story, the acacia branches hugging what had been my bedroom window. No light was on. A door from that bedroom opened onto a balcony where, if you waited quietly beside the tree, you could look birds and lizards in the eye. Once, absorbed in a nest taking shape, I'd heard a man call, "Be my wife!"

He'd been calling from the street, where I now stood. Flustered, I'd stared as he waved, laughing, missing a front tooth. He was very black and muscular, dressed only in baggy shorts, his chest gleaming. "Be my wife!" he shouted again.

"I can't!"

"Tell me yes!"

"Why?" It was a game.

"I bring you beautiful home, better than that one, many children, you be gettin' rich with me!" And he had spread his arms, baring his pale palms, pursing his lips.

The next day at school a girl had told me I was lucky I'd said no, because the moment you said "yes" to a Ghanaian you were bound by law for life, and for a while I kept imagining myself dragged into his compound, wrapped in robes, and forced to pound cassava. I knew, of course, that things could never go that far, and later I learned that Ghana had no such law or custom, but at the time we'd both liked the idea, I think, that one careless word could turn our lives inside out. Schoolgirl to wife, virgin to mother, white kin to black.

The movie sound track bubbled faintly; *Nero's* thumped. Adbul didn't wake as I sidled past. When I reached Independence Avenue, I took a few steps against the traffic, back toward the well-lit corner where people stood for taxis, and I'd barely flinched before one swerved to a stop. The driver quoted the regular fare and motioned me into the front seat. As we pulled out, I turned to nod at the other passengers, and then I saw my mistake—the wire rim glasses flush against that craggy face, the long limbs jutting. It was the man who'd yelled outside the annex. Cramped and watchful, he seemed about to spring.

"That's right," he said ominously. "You sit in front. White in front of black."

Directly behind me, his friend smiled lazily, head lolling, his shrunken chest and spindly wrists nothing like Kwame's. The third was missing. Hunched over the wheel, the driver accelerated, his massive, bald head purposefully fixed. Copying him, I stared ahead at tail lights.

"That's right, make yourself at ease."

Should I answer? Wisecrack, sneer? What would an African girl do?

"Always without worries, without cares, so high in your skyscrapers and airplanes, your homes like botanical gardens. Your father keeps you comfortable, isn't it? He puts gold on your fingers, and your mother hangs traditional masks in your parlor. I've seen your houses, I've been inside them to see. You think nothing can happen here because you are white. White people can't be poor in Africa. You never get our problems, there's nothing can touch that watery skin."

His breath was loaded with alcohol, but the window wouldn't open; the handle merely swung without engaging. We were racing along the usual route; nothing was really wrong. This was just a mistake, in a few minutes I'd step down, safe in my driveway. This man was no dingy crook; he wore stylish clothes, had money for a taxi, and, except for the few words he slurred, spoke the deliberate diction of the educated. Yet the raw edge to his voice made me squirm.

"You're a treasure, isn't that what you think, you're too precious for dirt to touch your skin, too white to have troubles? Your father acts so big but do you know why? Because my country is poor, because he's just a big man in a poor country. I can see him working in that bright office with lights in the ceiling and telephones. I can see your mother shopping, buying food imported in tins because ours is too dirty for your European stomachs! Your father must be so proud to give you this perfect life, to make you safe from any problems, but listen." Louder, faster, his words flew. "Your father is wrong. What if I gave you a problem right now, he would see. I could take you and fuck you dead on the ground, and when he came to find you, what could his money do then?"

"Stop," I said to the driver. "Stop here. Let me down." I couldn't stand that huge voice, the air swollen with his breath. Scooting forward, ready to bolt, I pulled a few cedis from my pocket.

"That's right." He grabbed the back of my seat. "Show him your money, and he'll do as you say. But not every Ghanaian is such a coward. Your money can't always keep you safe." He shouted at the driver then in Fanti, but we pulled over anyway and I tumbled out.

Planning to hail a new cab, I took several good strides before I glanced back. The men were slamming their doors, and the car swung into traffic, headed for me, I thought—but then it was gone. This didn't happen in Ghana; you heard about burglaries, corruption, people getting sick, but not this. Hardly poor, these guys were slick and brainy, out on the town. My arm outstretched to signal cabs, I ran.

The steps behind caught up and sprinted around so that my path was blocked.

"I could hurt you but I won't," he said. "I only want to talk. I want to hear about your perfect life."

Headlights swept past; I wanted to stay in their range. If I ran again I might wind up tackled in the dark. One hand flexing toward the traffic, I tried to reason. "What have I done to you? Why are you bothering me? I've never done anything to you."

He didn't answer. "This is my country," he said. "And I'm telling you what to do this time. I don't care how many cedis are in your pocket, I can make your life shit. I can hit you so hard you fall, I can take you here in the dirt. But I only want you on your knees. Get down on your knees."

His silent friend hung slightly apart, head slack. A taxi would stop soon. But no blue cars were in view. I lowered one knee to the ground.

"What if your father comes too late tomorrow? Put both knees on the ground." His arms rose like tentacles.

"Now you must tell me that you are shit and your father is shit and your mother is shit and England is shit and your life is shit. Tell me."

I knelt only for a moment, scanning the traffic as I mumbled, almost more afraid of being seen than of what might happen next. I felt foolish and weak, ashamed for not fighting back, and I thought of my father, calm and enduring, recessed behind dark lenses, as vulnerable as I.

Then blue flashed past, I hopped up, and brakes screeched as I sprinted for the door, jerking it open before the car had stopped. "Go!" I said, shutting myself inside. "Quickly, don't wait!"

The men, however, swayed where I'd left them, not bothering to follow.

"What happened?" asked the driver, shifting gears. He must have seen me kneeling. Sniffling, I willed my eyes dry, determined not to arrive home upset, not to let anyone there know how I'd cowered like a dog.

I told the driver, though, exactly what the men had said and done. He shook his grizzled head, grunted with indignation, nodded sympathetically, tugged at his ski cap. He was the kind of African I loved.

"Those men are bad," he said.

Monday morning Kwame rallied against the Ambassador. Waiting outside the fence, I studied Kwame's style, how his feet fell into place, the pock of contact in front of the body, the punch from the shoulder and high follow-through. I could do all that when the ball came straight to me, but I'd never tried to cover the court. Ambassador Whittier, for all his height, shuffled like mad before he stroked, twisting abruptly, adjusting his form to his bad timing. He always managed to score his points, and had won a trophy at that club, but he epitomized, I thought, the sort of impatient athlete who'd begun charging around before his swing could gel as second nature. Perhaps confidence could make up for shoddy form, but I didn't want to win that way.

Whittier crouched for Kwame's serve, something I'd never watched. Tinged brown with clay, the ball shooting straight up seemed to lift Kwame from the ground so that his feet dangled in the air when his racket hit. I thought of scissors snapping shut. The ball bounced just inside and whizzed past Whittier's awkward dash. Recovering with dignity, though, he pointed his racket at Kwame and said, "Wimbledon."

"You're easy on him," I said as Whittier drove off.

Kwame squeezed a fresh, white ball. "He's the Ambassador."

It could have been Kwame in that taxi, a different night, a different girl. Either way, I did begin to understand.

That Monday morning on Kwame's court I hovered beside the fence and wondered, "How can he not hate us?"

"What's wrong?" He bounced the ball for me to catch, and I looked at it, fuzzy and plush, tucked tightly in my palm.

"Cathy told me she wants to quit."

His jaw tilted up. "She has no patience, she never listens. I tell her to slow down, she's not getting it right, and she gets angry. Every time I give advice, she gets angry instead of listening. She's not for tennis."

"So when will I be ready to rally?"

"First you serve. Tomorrow you start serving."

"She thinks you're lazy, you know. That you like to stand in one place."

"You think so?"

"I think you're good."

"I'm good because I'm lazy." As he grinned, the black freckles appeared to lift above his skin.

"You don't really need the money, do you, or you'd teach Cathy what she wanted."

"Come on, let's go." He strode over to the net. "You're losing time. I won't go to Wimbledon, if you mean that."

He tossed and I swung, again and again; now and then I felt the impact in my soles. I had nothing else to say. But handing him a glass of water afterwards, I knew my lessons were spoiled. I might perfect my swing, learn to time my stride, even to serve with my feet in the air, but I could no longer pretend that we were friends.

What I'd really wanted for my money was this moment under the jasmine, when I could play hostess and Kwame guest, when I could lure him onto my turf. I'd been paying to dream of dancing with Kwame. I'd been paying for his hands brushing my back, nudging my elbow, his pressure on my wrist as we toed the baseline. I'd been paying him to tell me what to do.

As he guzzled the water, I watched his Adam's apple. He finished with his regular flourish, shaking the last drops onto the ground as Africans like to do, and wiped his mouth dry.

"When Cathy stops," he said, "your lessons can last one hour."

"If we rally."

He nodded, smiling, and although Cathy hadn't arrived yet I turned toward the house, leaving him alone on the bench.

We kept up the full hour lessons until summer ended, rallying and all; I improved, and Kwame stayed aloof, but I couldn't quit dreaming. The word for Kwame was "sexy." Who could guess what he was thinking, whose side he was on? Of course we didn't keep track of each other after I left; nobody did. Rochelle stopped sending Christmas cards the year she got married. I don't know where Cathy wound up; today we might be able to talk. I heard that when the Ambassador finished his appointment, Shirley Temple Black replaced him, which insulted the Ghanaians. They doubted that a child movie star could negotiate diplomacy.

My father said he was glad not to work under Ambassador Black, whether because of the sticky politics, or because he agreed with the Ghanaians, I can't say. Maybe if I asked him now, so many years later, he'd tell me the truth, but I don't, and I don't tell him my side, either. I can't remember the last time I saw him wearing sunshades, but they're always on him in my mind.

And I have to respect that man in the taxi. Everything about him was honest, from his wire rim glasses to his aching hate. Throughout the ride and roadside threats, he didn't touch me once.

Cropped

Mother is coming and all I can think of are the curtains. Paled by the sun, frayed to near lace. Do I like lace? Mother meant them youthful; when first hung, daisies the size of hands exploded into my kitchen.

That's Mother, scattering spurts of energy way over here, Sundi Village, the Republic of Zobola, Africa. Boxes keep coming. Her curtains arrived around November; now it's February and already they have aged. In the States I censored her zany tastes, perhaps put out the hot pink tablecloth when she brought pizza; that's all. Now I use everything. I've forgotten what I like.

Early on, new to Sundi, I had written her about the staring. Windows studded with eyes. After the AfricEd training center in Bashushi City, the teaching and language classes, the nights dancing with Stuart, Reg, Suzanne, and others, even after yearning for the two-year bush post all to myself, Sundi was a shock.

Scrutinized right now, I feel big. I draw the curtains open, stare back. Why do children never blink? Eyes like onyx, all pupil, they study me in my house, heads like domes suspended at the windowsill, mouths submerged.

"*Ntuka!*" I yell. Go away. They are gone, giggles trailing. In their place, the awful green shimmers. So emerald, so vast, framed by my mother's bleached daisies.

Curtains, she thought, would keep out eyes.

This is a river village. Below and west of our hill, the Zobola River stretches sky-gray between banks the color of malachite, and from the distance the floating clumps of mammoth-leaved vines look like islands. In the water, pirogues are splinters, barely visible, but you can hear the fishermen sing, paddles lapping.

This is forest, lots of bugs, fruit.

To the east, however, Sundi looks out over savannah — weeds and some brush that dry season withers from May to September. Savannah actually surrounds the river basin, west, east, north and south. Trees dot the expanse, baobabs the biggest. Hunched at the banks, the growth thickens with branches of all kinds clambering for light: wide-roofed acacias, palms, many I don't know.

Sundi's ferry separates the dirt road. We have some traffic; bush people on foot or bumping in lorries loaded with mangos and manioc for the Bashushi market, a day's drive. No *mundele* but me. The school is new.

Maybe a hundred kilometers upriver is Folo Dam, under construction. Rodney lays cable near Sundi with his team of ugly Americans afraid of niggers. He'll pop up, truck swinging a red cloud of dust, pull into a crowd of kids and throw them wet sodas from his cooler. "Red man," they call him. "Lydia, when is your red man coming?" I like how they say my name, two-syllabled, graceful. Rodney is tough-muscled Irish, wiry orange hair on his chest and forearms, too. He doesn't tan. I've never seen him wear a shirt. I've never seen him angry.

Water is what matters. Sundi has plenty. I carry my own at sunset, hike down to the women's source, a clean stream. There is a women's and a men's. The path is full at sundown, dawn also but I don't go then. I lug one ten-liter plastic bottle, sometimes twice. Mine is lime-green; the Chinese make them in garish colors my mother will like. Adolescent girls skitter straight-backed up the hill, balancing pails cushioned by cloth on their heads. The contest is to not spill. I lose. They say I am *mundele*, should have others carry for me.

I wonder what *mundele* means besides "white." I would have to learn Nituba inside-out and hear all the stories to understand. I'm getting better. Old Mrs. Sturk, still in Bashushi, who wouldn't leave with the rest of the missionaries, gave me a grammar book for Sundi's very dialect. The Twills at Mbataki wrote the large yellow pages of typed rules; I have the original. I hear about the *mindele* who came before: Doctor and Mrs. Twill from Mbataki Mission, and then, later, Gordon the AfricEd volunteer. I'm the first to live at Sundi.

One thing about *mundele*: the word belongs to the animal gender, not the people gender. The plural form takes the animal class prefix: *mindele*. The people plural prefix is "ba." *Batuba*. I live among the *Batuba* who speak *Nituba*. I am *mundele*. Animal.

February, flush in rain, lovely mud. Grassy savannah. Six months and I'm learning. At the source filling bottles, washing hair. When I take off my top, everyone stares. Little Mweni from next door pours the rinse as I bend at the waist, long hair pulsing in a wave.

Nights the forest envelops. As villagers tell stories at fires, I listen, picking up words. It's hard to hear laughter and not know why. Sounds are all rhythm: the insects' repeated crescendo, the random crack of burning logs. Drums. And the story, Nituba itself, the rolling slap of long-voweled syllables. Birds. I understand: *zolele* (love), *malembe malembe* (slow).

Classes are a separate world, all English, me in motion like behind television glass, students glued to seats. Rhythm is day-slowed to the brass bell punctuating each hour, the call and response pattern of oral drills. These young adult eyes are smaller than the kids' at my window, as if the bodies have grown up around. These eyes crinkle with laughter and blink when called on.

Some students are older than I, like Mayala, whose English is exceptional. He says his cousin Pili, big man in the city, tutors him. At school he uses words I never taught. "From a train, trees are a waterfall," he said during my transportation lesson.

"Yes!" I agreed, putting it on the board, seeing the blur. Classes are sometimes a dialogue between him and me. He is twenty-two; I'm twenty-one. Afternoons he tutors me in Nituba. Nights he drums for the storytellers.

This afternoon he comes with his drum. He has promised to teach me music.

"Everybody runs," he says in English, meaning the kids I chased from the window. I have closed the curtains again.

"My mother is coming," I say, rattling the blue aerogram. Will he understand?

"From America?" He amazes me, speaking English, respectfully dressed in a clean t-shirt and ironed jeans. With skirts to my calves, I dress carefully also. Women do not show much leg.

I've never liked my legs, how they are flabby-thighed without ankles. My knees are dimples. I'm not pretty, not in America. My ears stick out, my nose is a beak. My brother used to call me dumpy. *His* prima donna divorced him. My hair is best, thick and highlighted. But I'm better than beauty, than my mother's quick jabs to sit up straight and smile, her pumice stones and lotions, the snappy clothes she bought to pick me up so I'd get noticed.

What I want is knowledge, not fluff, not a nine-to-five job either. My college friends couldn't believe me in Africa, but look at them, pink-collar and bored. My old flame Gib in his lab, well paid, piling up possessions, sending me leftist literature. He's disappointed because he thinks I've sold out to neo-imperialism. He's just bought a Fiat. Presley, the cutesy woman he axed me for, does it justice.

Well, what would I do in the States? My degree is Global Studies, pretty vague. Pink is not my color.

From the floor I lift and roll the straw mat, proud that the earth worn to a polish is free of grit. Each morning before school, I sweep. At dawn the whole village quivers with brooms

98

swishing. I greet neighbors, rapas tied carelessly, from doors where we stand waving mats and rugs. Rose-tinted dust plumes.

My house is square mud, like everyone's. A row of teachers' quarters, cement huts, stands near the school, but I didn't want to be off alone, the only teacher to have arrived so far. So I took this house recently vacated by a family who moved to Bashushi. Urban migration is high.

Inside is like a villager's, black ceramic jugs of water cool in shadowy corners, curtains drawn against the sun. Furniture of wood, simple desk chairs, stools for relaxing.

Drum tucked under his arm, Mayala carries two stools and we go outside under a tree. He sets the stools on the mat, keeping feet clean of not-quite-dried mud from last night's rain. Now fast clouds blot out the sun. We watch them ride the crests of hills, fluid and evil.

Mayala gestures a story, mixing English and Nituba phrases. When the sun is strong, *ngolo* (knocking air with clenched fists, biceps pumping), the spirits run from clouds to go underground. But they cannot. We see these cowardly spirits as shadows caught skimming the earth's surface, like flies at screens.

Mayala removes his sandals and curls his feet snug around the drum's base. Hands thump flat, slowly. He points to his ear. I am to listen.

His ears are small and tucked. There is something compact about Mayala, the nose hugging his face, cheeks plump when he smiles. He's always smiling. I tell him so in Nituba. He smiles.

My hands are twigs in his as he shows how to tap, where the thumbs go. Does this mean something to Africans, this touching? It does to me.

When I play the drum, I'm happy at how slow I can be. A bird calls, a machine-gun fire of notes. The wood vibrates between my bare feet. The bird calls again. I play steady. I'm afraid to improvise.

It's so hot I cut my hair. Mayala hates it long, it frightens him in bed. Only Africans who are crazy grow their hair wild.

You see them in city streets, their long ropey strands falling unkempt as they sway on bent legs, eyes closed, chanting.

Outside, with a mirror propped in a branch, I test the scissors. I snip at air, watching the silver legs flash shut. First I clasp my ponytail and saw above the rubber band. The clump is thick. I saw endlessly. The sound reminds me of insects chirping. Why do I feel I'm killing something? Children surround me, clapping. I understand *mbote*, the word for good, happy, beautiful, healthy. *Mbote, mbote*, I hear. I hope they mean beautiful.

When the ponytail snaps free I hold it up, and the children fall back, reverent. Over a foot long, it puffs out at the end. It frightens me. I hang it from the branch, and hairs lift in the breeze.

A girl in a shirt and no underwear bursts forth to tag the end. Everyone squeals. "*Ntuka!*" I shout, waving the ponytail. They run, beige bottoms of feet flashing.

The rest is easy. For the front I look in the mirror, outlining tufts. My ears are free. The back I can't see, and don't care enough to borrow a mirror from next door. People will like it short, whatever the style. Feeling, I cut piece by piece close to my scalp, but not too close. My neck is free, cool, slightly naked.

I hear Rodney's truck ten minutes before he arrives. His is a high-geared purr, not the sputter of overloaded lorries. Mayala and I are in bed, sweating. This is fine with the villagers. Nobody stares at me with Mayala.

Since the March rains have eaten at the road, traffic has been sparse. From the door I see Rodney peering through his spattered windshield, rushing to a stop. Passenger Zobolans begin to climb down from the back, careful not to spill Cokes. I'm still knotting my rapa at my waist and tucking in my shirt.

"Your hair," he says, unfolding out of the cab, too big and white.

"Red man," I reply. He has just been to Bashushi and has gone by the AfricEd office for my mail. Two boxes, I see, and letters, and volunteer memos.

Mayala bangs shut the door and stands behind me.

"Well, I liked it better before," says Rodney, "but this is Africa."

I wait, worried he'll insult the Zobolans, that I'll get mad. I need him to drive my mother here in May. But he's not as bad as the other engineers I sent away. When they jeered at my lovely Sundi people, I ballooned with hate, yelling at them never to come back. One wanted to buy a girl, another chased the children with a switch blade.

Taking my letters and boxes, I introduce Mayala. As Rodney shakes hands he offers beer and asks to go inside because he's been out all day. With jerky politeness, not sure how to act, he stoops into the house, prattling on in his clipped eastern accent about supply shortages and hold-ups on the line, and about a barbecue at the Dam this weekend. I let him talk, the English sounds good.

"Where's the T.V.?" he jokes. "We got some good flicks ready for the weekend. You can't tell me you don't miss movies! Popcorn, Charlton Heston."

"I don't think so, Rodney." I wonder if Mayala understands, but he's sipping, enjoying the beer. "Can Mayala come?"

Rodney peers again, even though he's right across from me. He shifts his bulk around, uncomfortable on the stool, cowboy boots pointing out. I feel sorry for him trying to be sensitive. He's wrong here in this hut. Beside Mayala he looks crusty, creaky.

"I think you really ought to come," he declares. "Get back to your roots."

I smile at his humor, but say no. He can't understand me happy at Sundi. He wants white ass. Why don't I want a white man? I can see confusion in his leer. As he speaks of a trip to South Africa, civilization, his eyes are pale, empty of mystery.

We can be friends, it seems; he agrees to bring my mother. Can't I shut down school three days and come along? For my mother? He asks as if to strike a bargain.

"I'm on the national school schedule. We're not finished 'til June." I take my job seriously. Or do I just want to? I flinch as the familiar private question glimmers: what am I doing here? Teaching is, at least, better than Rodney. I glance at the curtains riffling above my gas camping stove.

I feel I've won something, until we say good-bye. Through the truck window comes his fleshy hand, grabbing the back of my head. I wish for my hair. He pulls me forward and whispers something corny: "Whenever you're ready." Bristly chin, humid breath on my face. He lets me go, spins away.

Inside one box is freeze-dried mountaineering food wrapped in *National Enquirer* pages. I laugh. Below part of an article about Johnny Carson is a half-page ad for some no-wrinkle cream. I spot two different ads for exercise devices. Zobolans don't think of fat and wrinkles; they want to eat, to get old. I laugh and laugh.

The other box is Christmas tinsel and angel's hair, three months late. There's a metallic cardboard star, too, to fold into three dimensions. Folding, I think of December in Bashushi, dancing at Pili's Golden Pot with Stuart, Neddie, Christine, anyone, all the prodigal volunteers assembled for vacation in the capital to share new knowledge. For summer we plan a beach trip. That will be after Mother. I envy Jane and Max at Kibundu, a suburban town with electricity. The gold star goes above the kitchen window. I drape tinsel on the curtain rods.

I've invited Mayala for a freeze-dried dinner. Usually his mother cooks for him—palm-oil beans and manioc, fish stew—but I've told him this is special. For him, I've pounded the manioc paste because to Zobolans nothing is food without this fou-fou. We feast on beef stroganoff, dipping fou-fou with our fingers. He can't believe the meat.

"What is this American meat? How can this be in that box?"

"I add water. In America it's frozen, the water is removed, so it's dry. They put it into packages."

He swallows happily. "*Mbote*. But why? You don't have live meat, still strong, fresh dead?"

"We do. But they make this certain kind for camping. Vacations in the forest, mountains, away from the city."

This is a hard concept. To Mayala anything but the city is bush, farming, manual labor, boredom. I explain mountain climbing and smog. Bad air. *Mpasi*: bad, ugly, sad, difficult.

"But why don't you hunt on the mountain? Meat in the city but not the forest?"

"Yes."

"Me, I'm going to the city. Bashushi."

The stroganoff is finished, the bowl wiped smooth with fou-fou, so I pile the dishes outside in buckets, to wash later. If it rains, I'll find them soaking.

When I serve the strawberry pudding, Mayala asks, "This is meat also?"

"Taste."

"This one very good," he nods. "But you know I will go to Bashushi. With Rodney. This living here is bad, too quiet. My cousin Pili will help. A real school."

"You should go," I say. The tinsel winks in the gas lamplight. After all, this is why I like him. He's smarter than a village farmer. His younger brothers are big enough to care for his parents.

"You come also." Pink pudding foam streaks his lip.

"I like it here."

"This I don't understand. What do you do here? *Mundele* alone, so young, *mbote*."

Pretty? It's the haircut, I think. He goes on, "Why do you want to be poor?"

He keeps me thinking for days. I decide he's decided I'm useless. His cousin Pili can help him more. I decide this is good, I don't want to be a missionary. Yet every so often something in me knots up solid as a kola nut, deep under my chest at a place that feels like my center. Whether it's anger or sorrow I'm not sure; it has something to do with love, I think, although when I think of Gib the knot disintegrates with how good I feel to be the one, this time, to say no.

Mayala is sweet, he keeps tutoring; my Nituba improves. I begin to follow fireside stories. Many are about the missionaries and *mundele* power. How Pili got rich.

May. The savannah browns, the air cools. Mother has come and gone, vibrantly splashing through Sundi.

The dry lightning plays at night. I sit on a rock, the village behind, the river behind that. As the savannah rattles in wind, I imagine weeds grown tall swaying, but it's too dark to see. The sky is a light show with repeated patterns of lightning, a flash north, then south, north. Electric veins fork, spanning cavernous clouds. They never connect with earth.

I'm safe. But I feel caught. I hear drumming; the stories are beginning. Someone new drums; Mayala has left with Mother and Rodney.

She was happy to see me with men. But she liked the children best, spent all four days juggling babies. Her visit was a brief detour from her trip to Paris with my father, where he was attending a trade conference. "Delighted, Lydia," she kept bubbling. "So happy to see you happy."

The villagers loved her. Ecstatically wide-mouthed, she was up to her waist in children, passing out Lifesavers, hairpins, anything in her purse.

"Lydia," she said one afternoon, Mweni in her lap. Mweni had Christmas tinsel braided into her hair, like a caricature of my mother's grey streaks. "That Rodney is nice."

"Yes."

A pause, she looked down at her sandals. I knew what she was thinking, that he was good for me, a good catch. "Mother, I'm not trying to be you."

I cringe thinking how it sounded, gravelly with disgust and impatience. It seems I don't speak any language so well. When she looked up, tiny wrinkles twitching at her pursed lips, I started to cry, furious at my tears, at the confusion squishing all my pride and purpose, that had made me want to hurt her.

"What are you trying to be?" she asked calmly.

I shook my head. I shake my head now, hard. These are her tactics: follow me to Africa, make me feel wrong, helpless, ugly. And then I see her so white, Mweni on her lap, and Mother looks old, thick arms sturdy around Mweni on her lumpy lap;

that one moment emblematic of a life spent mothering. How could that be enough?

The lightning flickers, silent. I listen to the weeds' friction in wind, the bugs, the drums. By September the landscape will be charred, airborne ash will tickle nostrils, air tinged with incense. Slash and burn is how they farm. They say five hundred years ago this savannah was forest. It strikes me that if all the farmers were to leave, the trees would grow back.

Hymns

Stella knew that returning to the States would distort her soul, and she had reached a point where knowing was enough, without explaining, even to herself. She knew that Africa was home. The smooth black children in the brilliant dust, village to village, were her own vast family. Her husband Phillip craved his sisters and father, that she understood; he missed everybody speaking English and the telephones. Nine years and his work here was done. "Done!" he would say, as if a tennis match were over.

Stella didn't play tennis anymore, had never been too good. Early on, Phillip had taught mission Africans. Now that other missionaries had come, however, he played most often with Lloyd Brendle, doubling sometimes with the Dufts. The abandoned African protégés waited until the single court Phillip had built was free, then knocked at Stella's door to borrow racquets for their own games.

While Phillip played Lloyd this afternoon, the Jituba Mission Mamas' Choir was meeting at the church. This squat rectangular building, perched so severely above the houses and schools, bloomed with good when the choir practiced. Stella was again first in the church; she suspected that the African wives waited at their homes until they saw her climbing the hill. Through the window she glimpsed, amidst tall weeds, a clump of women waddling up draped in multicolored rapas, babies tied to their backs. She sat on a wood bench and quizzed herself from the dirty pile of typed lyrics tattered at the corners. As she stared, the Ifili words swelled and moved forward off the paper. They were in her head now by heart. Today she would not read, she'd watch Raphael directing, his black hands held out flat, rising and falling like ocean rafts.

People began to arrive, nodding and scuffing over to shake Stella's hand and fill her bench. She lay her text by her feet as Raphael hurried past the pews to his place in front. Always in flux, between points, he slanted ahead with stooped shoulders, heels trailing. His Western slacks and shirt were curtains that his elbows and knees prodded from within. While singing, he would rock side to side as if seeking his center of gravity.

Before the dozen or so women were settled, Stella caught what she called his private smile, for her only. His face made her think of the moon—impossibly round, effervescent with its spherical dimensions intuited rather than evident to the naked eye—yet with skin so black, certainly the dark side of the moon.

From the church the tennis *pock* was irregular, dissonant against the throats clearing and chairs scraping while Raphael flipped through his hymns. He thought she had forgotten her copies, Stella realized when he waved one sheet and came towards her. "No, thank you," she said then in Ifili. "No need."

"No?" He flashed his public smile; it slid from her across the whole group. "Mrs. Osborne knows Ifili too well!"

The Mamas chorused. "Ay-ee!"

"Anh-HAH!"

The brass triangle clanged. Used to these occasions when all faces turned for her response, she sat up straight. The women watching had brown skin and large teeth in grins so wide their cheeks bulged. They expected her usual English, which they all understood but did not use among themselves.

Stella's Ifili vocabulary was small. "Your language is heaven."

A communal sigh, cheers, and everyone turned back to hear what song from Raphael, what pitch. Stella was alto; in fact her voice tended to stray and she'd always avoided singing. Typically the preacher's wife led a choir; as a newcomer she had refused that honor. Last year, though, around the time Phillip had brought up leaving, she had joined the Mamas' Choir. He called it a whim, joked about rampant boredom and how she needed out—next she'd be tying a stuffed cloth to her back, going "Mama" on him, and that hurt because Stella really did want a child.

With the women pressed skin to skin on two benches, shoulders swaying left and right together, domes of infant heads gently lolling, and with Raphael more moonlike than ever, his lips pursed like a shadowed crater, Stella knew boredom had not motivated this off-key effort. Being a part, a mere one of many, was a revelation after so much leading and teaching. For too long she had stood alone, floating from one audience to another as if in a bubble of logic. Boil water, wear shoes, abstain, abstain. She had stalked the fronts of classrooms handing out things and collecting, inching her words across chalkboards. The blanket of African faces was always over there, apart. Whatever she could tell them they had already learned but she could not say simply that her work was done. Something lingered to draw her in among them.

The women around Stella sang loudly as metallic percussions pricked the wailing melody and the tam tams rolled. Not yet, but when they got going they would stand, sway and shuffle in unison and Raphael would dance to show the prayer was hot. Raphael's dance was a puzzle: how, barely moving, he was so full of motion. When he danced his wide eyes appeared to see nobody, not even Stella, although his pupils pulled at her like magnets.

He was thirty-two, too young for her, but then Phillip lately was too old. Spindly, his skin grey except for the pink that mottled his mouth, nose and skull up where his brown hair had receded, Phillip had faded. She was sure she'd loved him once as the tall adamant student whose vim would help the poor. After her church childhood she had been ready for Africa. Without parents she'd been lucky to be educated; the Baptists had put her through college, a small one where no dancing was allowed, where she'd found Phillip's horizons enthralling. She'd been ready and wanted her work to help. Whether or not it had was no longer an important question.

The women were rising now, Raphael's hands over his head, and the rocking melody washed Stella to her feet, and the mass of bodies connected her to the ground so she wouldn't drift on up and over into Raphael's pliable arms. She'd been in them before, once, so far once. That had been during last month's outing of the Mamas' Choir to Oyo where they sang for a sister mission. On a Saturday they'd arrived in town stiff from the hours bouncing in the Jituba truck over sparse savannah, had eaten rice and stew in the mission's bare meeting room, had then been shown their rooms to wash off the bush dust and sleep. Stella accepted a private room and, after smearing her dirt film with water from a basin, sat staring at a network of cracks in the plaster wall, wondering if Raphael would come, if that slow grip and release of her elbow, the way his fingers singed her breast, had been a message and if she'd answered it correctly, squeezing her arm to wedge his hand there, just a second. No one saw. His eyes had been narrow, so deep the whites hardly showed.

A final clang. This song had ended, the refrain repeated until the syllables were a percussion of gibberish. Singing this way let out something in Stella, her thoughts impulsive as the instinctual tweak of hips. People whistled and clapped; some blew out, exhaling like horses. A good song. Raphael asked if they wanted to sit before starting the next one, but no one did. The dancing had begun.

"The world must dance," Stella announced, and the women squealed and yipped. She wondered if being drunk felt so airy and fast.

Marla, the woman on Stella's left, poked her, saying, "You dance very well, like an African!"

Stella nodded thank you and steadied herself to concentrate on the new hymn's lines. The stanzas dragged on, the women restrained until the chorus. Still slung to their mothers' rocking backs, the babies slept. The heat gelled around the perspiring crowd, a residual heat left by the sun ducking below the corrugated school roof. Years ago, the tropical humidity had been an obstacle, the sunlight spikes in Stella's eyes, but she had grown into the climate, noticing its consistency more than the sweat trickling down her back. Perhaps her weight loss was a form of acclimation—she remembered having felt so bulbous, oozing at the folds of flesh around her middle. Perhaps her stomach flattening gradually, her jaw angling out, was her personal adaptation. Yet if she could have chosen, she would have grown huge as the African women proud of eating, fleshy and fecund.

Phillip didn't mind not being a father, she knew. He was a father anyway, his congregation of surrounding villagers successfully devout and educated, his replacement, Lloyd, poised for the new era of expansion, the dispensaries, water pumps, tennis courts sprouting across the bush.

Chanting was taking hold. The refrain reduced to rhythm lost literal meaning, and Stella wondered if the words fractured into noise took on power that everyone but she understood. What was this incantation, what were they asking, and of whom? This message was not for Stella's God, not his language. Whatever they were asking, Stella wanted too.

Bony, recessed between bulky matrons, she was no more than the pulse between the real people, the dancing singers. Their message rippled across her ribs so she bounced from the balls of her feet, lifting, so she knew about being alive, solid on the floor yet full of sky. For life, they were praying, for more of the same and better, loving the concrete, skidding, loving better the red soil and rains and digging up manioc roots grown fat to cook. The leaves and insects poking from everywhere they loved so much they, too, gave birth abundantly: the more crowded the earth the better.

She believed their prayer and imagined pastel spirits huge and diaphanous, folding like silk around her God, an angry little humanoid splayed helpless against heaven like an insect specimen against glass. He had not heard her. He was useless, had not given her a child, had ignored even her big sin. Ever since her tryst with Raphael, as a matter of fact, she'd felt twinges of happiness and wisdom. Not a whimper, not a spasm from that old God.

Late at night back in Oyo when she'd heard the cautious knock, she'd actually thanked God and let Raphael in quickly before anyone saw. His lanky arms wrapped around and compressed her to a tight fit, perfectly snug; there would be no room for anyone bigger. He was strong enough to keep her heart from flying or her bones from exploding as he squeezed to lift her onto the bed when her muscles were going liquid. It was all slow, and what Stella remembered was his eyes pouring into hers; she could not look at anything else, and all the summer blaze inside seemed, oddly, to shoot through those copper eyes and her own.

The chant held on, too long. Stella suddenly wanted to stop singing and be still but could not avoid bumping along. The sun was down, a blue dusk spreading. The tennis game would be over and the choir would break up, only two songs practiced — but with pure rendition. No program could guide honest singing.

At home, Phillip said he'd heard from the court the choir practice, that today's music had been unusually robust. Stella smiled, glad for the habitual silence he knew her by, glad she didn't need to answer. Later, unable to sleep, she slanted away from him and let the chorus echo, listening for clues. How could she leave? But practically, how could she not? Phillip's breathing squeaked methodically from where he lay crumpled, so loose in his skin. These days his vacant touch was like birds alighting, taking off. His power was in words, in voiced decisions.

He had decreed the people could dance so that he could preach to a full church, yet he himself never felt the rhythm. With a separate impulse his head would jerk and nod at his singing congregation, then stall. Raphael's power, however, was in his heart. Not blocked by logic or decision, his lure was an inadvertent gift the same as blood pumping was a gift. Raphael could make her fertile, Stella knew. She could be his second wife, or third; perhaps he already kept a second wife in a village, one who would welcome Stella, the mission's exiled sinner. Coddled and spoiled, parented by the whole village, she would love them all.

Tight in Raphael's imagined grip, she slept, but in her dream his pressing face was that of her old God's, but black: a frail and furrowed night bearded with clouds, eyeless. She peered into the sockets and saw woman after woman, all dark and buxom, none of them her. She woke before dawn, chilled and worried. Phillip lay on his back, his breath whistling. If she was, in fact, a sinner, she would be punished by Raphael's indifference. The possibility loomed like her dreamed specter, then shrank against the bedroom wall, reduced to a fizzling nightmare. He did, he must love her: only honesty could pierce so beautifully. Her old God was wrong, crippled by his barren sky. Africa's pull still held.

She realized that if she told Phillip with stern calm that they must divorce because she was staying behind, not for mission work but for herself, so she might grow, he would think her insane. In her mind she saw him angry, not hurt. If she could have pictured him sad and damaged, she might have changed her mind. She tried and could not.

Raphael didn't know she was leaving the day she packed mostly cash in a basket and put her walking shoes over socks and followed the road out. A few Mamas on their way to fields waved, asking where she was going. She told them for a walk. "Anh-HAH," they laughed, as if they knew exactly where she was going even if Stella didn't. She would walk a while and catch a truck to the train, ride it deep into bush and stick in some remote spot until after Phillip was gone. In a note, she'd made clear her plan to stay, but she knew he'd come looking. If he found her — which was likely since she was conspicuously pale and anyone asked would say she'd been past — if he discovered her safely contented in a village hut, starting a garden, he might believe and leave her alone.

The road was densely packed dust, slim sheets picked up and disintegrated by a breeze. She was moving not over but through the road, embedded, inhaling clouds of soil like smoke. Her nostrils burned. Raphael she would see again although she had told him nothing, afraid he'd lose his job as mission assistant if Phillip found out. She'd return to see finally what Raphael's eyes said.

She would learn to read these eyes and chants, and forget about the words. Swinging her basket, Stella remembered the last choir practice. At the end she had bent down for the typed lyrics. The paper was scattered in shreds, smudged and punched apart by the stomping feet. And now, walking, she could not recall a single line. She hummed. The chants that happened dancing, that came up from below the toes, told and asked best.

The
Marabou Shed

From above, the airplane's shadow was a tiny cross
skimming the forest. A river glimmered like a scar.
According to her father, who was working the con-
trols, Jeremiah Susan Randolph knew nothing. She sat
gazing at the endless green. Effaced by the droning wind
and engine and the fickle needles of the instrument panel
as intimate to him as his own aviator brain, she was in-
clined to agree. Yet she preferred her private void to his
hellish barbed-wire grid of right and wrong; she was
starting from scratch. His home at Baku Mission was an
ideal spot for moral confusion because if she could just
avoid his goggle stare she could immerse herself in jungle to dress scantily, pit herself against the mosquito's
zooming sting, and play with the pygmies until her
elemental soul bloomed.

College had been wrong and stifling and she had
failed her first year triumphantly, crashing back to
Bryce Randolph's world of faith and airplanes to con-
front his steamy glare. They both referred to her stay as
a visit although she had not thought ahead to leaving, to
where or how, let alone when. Her letters had made
clear that school was "no go," that her summer holiday
might fizzle to limbo.

Jerry had expected the ticket home, as well as the initial brittle hug in the Bashushi airport, his bright arms jerking against her as if bumped in the hustle of Africans clearing customs. She had expected also her father's accusing silence. They had taken off for Baku right away in his tiny bush plane, and once during the hours in air she had tried to make him talk. Shouting above the motor, she started to say she knew he was mad, but he had cut her off: "You know nothing!"

There was nothing to explain, then, she reasoned. And he had no questions, not even at home, the plane cooling in its hangar. He did not ask, merely regarded her with angry worry from across the dinner table, his grey eyebrows fixed like stunned caterpillars, his thin lips parted like a wound. Behind him, rain smacked leaves like huge paws against the screened window.

"I could learn to fly," she said. Randolph had been training African pilots for eight years without teaching Jerry. His operation was small, with the red dirt runway and two light Cessnas, one trainer and one transport, but his purpose was part of the Baptists' attempt to develop the nation's infrastructure. Dispersed throughout the country were five instruction stations linked by two-way radios.

Chewing intently, he pursed his mouth to one side as if something were caught between his teeth. He swallowed, ducking his head, then answered. "How can you fly if you can't manage college?"

"You don't need a degree to fly a plane. Here you don't even need a license."

She watched his Adam's apple jump, disappointed that was all. She wanted a reaction, and had thought her remark a good slur on his purpose, his struggle to establish nationwide standards for flight certification. Randolph's lack of response infuriated Jerry; the horror of her father's ethics was that they were secret, that she was constantly in danger of snagging on invisible barbs.

Once she had come home wearing a gold cross. She knew he hated jewelry, had told a ninth-grade boyfriend no, she would have to hide a ring, and the boy had given her a necklace

she could wear always, that could not offend her father. Yet
even a simple cross was taboo; Randolph yelled to take it off.
She did, confused, young enough to want to please. Maybe he
knew she had a boyfriend, that the necklace was not a gift from
a girl, as she'd lied. Eventually she deduced that he hated the
Catholic manner of glitter and ritual, as if religion made pretty
was false. She remembered his huffy sulk when, in first or second grade, she had wished aloud that their church had madon-
nas, rosaries and saints, the way her friend Becky's did. Jerry
loved precious objects. Having forgotten the boy's name, she
still wore his cross sometimes, as a talisman.

She was wearing it now, wondering why she could not fly.
Punishment? Her father would not explain. Voice tight, he
nearly coughed his decree: a kernel "no" squeezed out through
silence.

Behind the calm angles of his nose, jaws and temples, who
knew what was brewing: love or hate, murder or sorrow? His
skewering eyes were all she had known since childhood when
she had craved and craved his lap to crawl into, or just his big
hand to hold. Running toward his knees she would stop and tot-
ter when she saw the face stony with warning.

At nineteen Jerry couldn't believe she was so bad, that he
believed she was. Had he been like that with her mother? Was
she like her mother? She had never asked, afraid the idea would
either buckle him like a boy or open the throttle to craziness.
Her mother had died of cholera in Bolivia when Jerry was three.

After her mother's death, Jerry and her father had lived in
Seattle with a series of housekeepers while he was a commercial
pilot, often out of town. That America was a blur of rain and
television, nothing like last year's shock, when the American su-
permarket aisles brimming obscenely with spangled packages
had frightened her. What was all that for?—the body needed
only so much. Those stockpiles of preserved goods seemed to
Jerry an irrational hedge against nuclear disaster, as if people
might really be alive to open cans on radioactive land.

Since arriving in Africa at the age of eleven, pygmy height,
and shuttling between months in the capital where she lived at

the mission center and attended the American school, and vacation months at her father's Baku outpost, Jerry had thrived on rice and beans day after day, on the rolls made in tall mud ovens, on dingy margarine that never melted, on the fruit. Bunches of finger-length bananas. Papaya, pineapple, mangoes, breadfruit, *nsafu*—like huge lavender olives—and oranges; she thought of this organic abundance as a benevolent avalanche, a spray of peanuts like falling rocks.

In high school, however, she had savored the luxury of imported potato chips. These she accepted from the non-mission kids whose parents lived in the city and worked for the U.S. government or Pan American or Exxon; they told her she didn't act missionary and invited her to their air-conditioned homes where she regarded herself in full-length mirrors. Her figure was the rare sort favored by the tropics; she borrowed tank tops and halters and very short shorts so her long muscles were as visible as possible. Even in pre-rain heat she sweated gracefully, her gold cross flat against her damp, cool sternum.

For this homecoming dinner she had dressed honestly, exactly as she would away from Randolph. Yet she was hurt that he asked no questions about her V-neck blouse, her necklace, her new blatancy. Patches of airy clothing lay waiting in her suitcase; in them she would assert her true self. Methodically chewing, Randolph asked no questions about her college behavior or her plans. He did not even comment when she mashed banana slices into her roll, sprinkled on top the peanuts roasted in their skins, and then dabbed on *pili pili* hot sauce before closing the roll like a sandwich.

Deemed incapable of flying, Jerry decided to build. She could have commissioned work from Amosi, Baku Mission's pygmy carpenter, who idled along between the minor repairs of broken hospital beds or school desks, but she wanted to learn. She found him outside his carpentry shop curled asleep in the fetal position, red baseball cap across his face. As she approached he lifted his round head; his immediate smile contradicted his half-open eyes and half-sitting pose.

"Jerry is back," he said, snapping to his feet, pressing finger-tips against his forehead as if willing himself clarity. "You want I get *nganja?*"

Amosi's people gathered potent wild hemp and smoked con-stantly when settled at camp between hunts; since high school Jerry had been a customer. Occasionally, if they were camped nearby, she would follow Amosi through the forest, skirting roots and creepers, sighting among the elaborate dapple of foli-age the flash of monkeys in branches; as his guest she would visit the temporary pygmy village.

Today she wanted something else, she told him, shaking his doll hand. "We have real work. I want to build many cages, and a little house like the Pastor's chicken shed. Do you have time?"

"Chicken shed," he repeated, nodding. "If Pastor, Doctor, someone want something, I stop, finish after."

That was fine since they both knew the mission's pace, that only her father worked all day every day, that the African mis-sion officials enforced little urgency. The Western presence had dwindled after all institutions, even religious, had been national-ized. Baku's hearty Bantu pastor welcomed the white pilot as an instructor and air chauffeur, a good liaison to the capital, and Jerry's father did not mind his lack of authority. He was not by nature a preacher, she had surmised, although what did keep him here in "the Interior," as the city people said, she was not sure. He puttered diligently in his hangar, attending his aircraft and students, lifting off for brief test flights, all to engineer some vast technological network beyond the forest's domain.

Building materials abounded. Amosi had chicken wire left-over from an earlier project. Cheap wood was trucked in from the nearby town and charged, with Jerry's signature, to the mis-sion. Amosi brought the equipment to a corner of her father's hangar and helped her build, first, several four-foot-square cages, for animals. Amused by her project, he laughed and jabbered, limber arms pointing and demonstrating.

Now and then she spotted her father lurking like a hunter behind an imaginary line, trying to figure her out, as if she were alien and dangerous. Or she might glimpse him mid-stride, the flash of his blue work shirt like a huge unpupiled iris.

After she had completed four cages to Amosi's six, they moved outside to erect a shed behind her father's bungalow. The site was just within the boundary of cleared brush, close to the forest shade.

"Let's see, room for ten cages, one side open to the trees, there, like the hangar, you know, only no sliding door, and room for me to sit inside, room for a chair and table. Oh, and storage, for feed and cleaning and that stuff. We can put a barrel outside for water."

Amosi stood doubtfully, a sturdy middle-aged knot of durable musculature fixed on the lawn by his red baseball cap. He tried to imagine. "All for chickens?"

"No, no, god no." When he smiled, knobby-cheeked, Jerry guessed that he knew the scripture about the Lord's name in vain. She went on, "Small mammals. Or anything. But not chickens."

"Rabbits? Those very good to eat. Make more anyway, no trying, more babies. More cages. More work for me." He waved a carpenter's level, the bubble constant in the slanting liquid.

"No, not rabbits, I don't think. I want a monkey. And a snake, and a parrot, and one of those skunk cats, a sphynx, or cervix, or serval, or something."

"We can get," said Amosi.

Jerry realized that to him pets would be strange, animals just for holding. To him all animals were protein, except humans and perhaps his totem. One of her college books had discussed totems, how some primitive clans worshipped the spirit of an animal, plant, or other thing as an ancestral emblem. If a clan had descended from a green mamba that snake would protect each member, never biting. Jerry wanted a totem. What spirit had spawned the Randolphs? A bird, probably, it felt like a bird.

When little, Jerry had tried to conjure her guardian angel by deliberately falling off her bike, expecting her fall to be broken by electric silky arms, as if the velvet smile and lightning hair might be her mother.

"Do you have a totem?" she asked Amosi.

"Sorry?"

"A totem, a special spirit that protects your clan."

"I don't understand." He had not moved. The forest behind him sloped upward from brush, narrow huge-leafed stems and spiralling roots thick as her waist, to emerald froth hovering a hundred feet above like an arrested tidal wave.

When her eyes dropped back to meet Amosi's, his glistening bewilderment entangled in the whole forest of his heart, her determination soared. To be so uncomplicated, so in tune that life's meaning escaped false labels! Jerry believed she would realize herself among the animals harbored in her shed, where she would listen, watch, commune.

Suddenly impatient, she shouted, "So let's go, build build, work work!"

Amosi yipped, grinning, and threw her the level, pointing her where to go.

Rain hampered the shed's progress, smashing down in spurts any time of day, pummeling the black tarps bulging over lumber and tools. If dawn came pink and dry they began that early; if not, they waited to squish through a shower's leftover film. Bit by bit they sawed and planed, then hammered boards into place, sawdust and the resiny aroma of fresh unfinished wood mingling with the fetid sweetness of the decomposing forest floor. Yet when the noon air began to heave with humidity they slowed, stopping finally when everyone was crawling off to dream, asleep or not, reclined on beds, chairs, or shaded straw mats.

Some afternoons Jerry walked the mission stoned and felt herself singly alive among the figures lounging at doorways and under trees, all frozen in time. She was in a *Star Trek* episode, she dreamed. The weight of her lighter and pipe clinking in the pocket of her cut-offs, so short the pocket poked a fat white tongue below the sparse fringe, was instead a communicator; she could summon Spock any moment and they could fall in love, zapping everyone else back to life. He would leave her, of course, or better, she him.

She had watched *Star Trek* daily on the dormitory television at college. She had also read, beginning each semester by attending the first of about ten different classes and affixing all the syllabi to her mustard-colored walls. Then instead of attending classes and exams she had read as much on the reading lists as the library provided, spending her book money on hash and clothes. Evenings she had entertained classmates, drilling them on what she'd missed, invariably satisfied that she'd missed nothing. Often she'd keep a boy overnight—she could not think of them but as boys—whom she would throw out before morning so she wouldn't have to see his soft acned cheeks and deluded exuberance.

Thus Spock kept Jerry company as her equatorial afternoons crystallized in fantasy. Mornings she watched Amosi perch on precarious angles of the developing shed. After self-conscious dinners with her father, the conversation limited to his terse outlines of immediate flight obligations, she hid in her room with books from his shelves while he worked in some other private corner. She guessed that his Christian principles deterred him from telling her to leave, to quit living by whim. Then when the shed was finished she saw him even less, appearing sometimes at his dinner table, sometimes not, leaving his cook in a flurry of indecision she soothed by saying, "All I need is the rolls and fruit, nothing special."

Fruit was what she ate, alone in the shed as she absorbed the wise green. When the unpredictable rain roared metallically on the iron roof the shed darkened so that she lit the storm lamp hanging from a hook above the table stacked with aviation manuals. Soon her first pets, two sullen parrots procured by Amosi in town, shared one cage, and their rank silence permeated the musty gloom. Jerry loved them as much as the rain drumming.

Meanwhile, Bryce Randolph flew, circling quickly with a trainee, or off on longer trips to distribute medical supplies to scattered dispensaries, or to chauffeur the Pastor to his village. Every month or so, Randolph made the long flight to Bashushi and stayed a while, stocking provisions; there would be paperwork and meetings with withered fellow pilots at Baptist head-quarters. So he warned Jerry, one night over the elephant stew served so proudly by the cook—a recent pygmy hunt had downed this marauding village-stomper—that he would be gone several days; would she like to come?

His tone was businesslike, indifferent, and he studied his plate as if the answer would emerge from the stew. Jerry smiled, chewing extensively on the gamey meat, and refused, said she liked it there at Baku. He had relied on the mission center to discipline her in high school, to dress and feed her properly. She thought of the soupy yogurt, the bony women, hair short and dull, the dorm-style room she'd shared with other kids and said, no, thank you. Someone awful would certainly comment on her skimpy clothes, offer her work, push her toward their purpose.

The morning he left, she woke wrapped in her damp sheets surrounded in blackness, the muffled scrapings and shouts of flight preparation drifting from the hangar through her window. The sun felt hours away; she knew more than saw the bedroom shapes, had for years memorized the bureau and hanging face mirror, the bookshelves and wicker hamper. Nothing had changed. She pictured the huge bamboo cross claiming the wall above her headboard and sat up to peek through her slatted window at the hangar's electric glow.

She drifted down to her shed, feeling with her toes the path pressed trip after trip by her own feet, once inside lighting the lamp to read a chapter: "Taking Off and Landing." The pages were tinged orange with dawn before she realized she was reading without the lamp's aid and blew it out. Then the air trembled as her father opened the throttle, the noise receding as he taxied down the runway, building again to shake the shed walls as he careered up to lift off, banking like a vulture over the roof. Jerry shut her eyes and felt the wings rising, rising as the parrots shrieked.

Then silence descended, she turned pages, the morning wore on as if echoing an act of god, and the parrots glared, rocking side to side. Eventually the jungle compelled her to slam the book; she stared ahead until the leaves blurred, concentrating on the monkeys' hooty screeches and the birds bickering above the insects' chorus. Occasionally a branch crashed.

Later she heard footsteps, and, expecting Amosi who visited often with apologies for not finding new animals, she was surprised when a white man loomed up, blocking her forest.

"I missed him," he said. American, he looked, in corduroy slacks and a ripped t-shirt, hair scalped to a blond fuzz, a backpack riding his shoulders. His face poured toward the end of a nose that reminded her of a lopped elephant trunk.

Having spoken so seldom this summer, she didn't know what to say.

After a moment, he tried, "The pilot's your father, isn't he? A guy in the hangar told me you were here." Then, "You speak English, don't you?"

"Where did you want to go?"

He smiled, reassured, teeth dim and even. "Upcountry." Leaning to drop his pack, he went on, "Think he might give me a ride? I heard he flies cargo."

"And you're cargo." She saw him itemized on her father's flight inventory: 2' by 6', 160 lbs., contour adjustable, fragile.

Without the weight of his pack he seemed to expand. He expanded toward her, climbing a couple of steps to lean over the threshold of the raised floor. "Mind if I come in?"

She cleared a place where he could sit on the table.

"What'cha got in here? Parrots, huh? Polly wanna cracker?" He tapped the cage.

"Huh?" echoed one.

This was the first she'd heard the parrots talk. She said nothing, watching him tap again. "Huh, huh?" he repeated. "So what's the rest of the cages for? More parrots? A choir, you could have, train them to sing together."

He seemed to like hearing himself talk, more interested in his own ideas than her information. Jerry imagined him little, inside one of the cages.

"I'm trying to get upcountry, to the mountains. I'm on my way out of Africa, but the long way, checking out the rain forest and the pygmies." He sat heavily on the table; luckily Amosi had designed it sturdy. "I was teaching, over by the coast in Semba, for two years. How long have you been here?"

This answer he waited for; Westerners in Africa defined each other by time. Two-week visitors differed from two-year contractors; both differed from lifers.

"My father's been here eight years. I was gone last year to school in the States."

"You lived out here seven years?"

"No. I went to school in Bashushi City. How did you get this far?" She wondered how hot his sunburned neck would feel against her fingertips.

"Your doctor here gave me a ride; I was hitching from town. I came from Bashushi on the riverboat, six days on the river. Now it's trucks out to the mountains unless your father gives me a lift. I'd like to avoid those pokey trucks. Is your father headed that way anytime soon?" Clutching his knees were mud-caked knuckles.

"He might go to Fufalba. Is that where you want to go?"

"Where's that?"

This man smelled, Jerry decided, both acrid and saccharine; she likened the odor to passion. He probably hadn't washed since boarding the boat. She stood, pulling at her shorts which had rolled up as she sat.

"Come on to the house, you can wash and eat. You can stay until my father gets back, Thursday probably. Then you can talk to him about Fufalba. He hasn't gone there in a while, he might be planning something."

Passing the parrots' cage, she stopped. "Huh," she said, and waited. The four seedlike eyes stared with their same odd, surprised look.

What Jerry loved about Max was the avid irresponsibility with which he bulldozed each day and night. Nonchalantly ugly, he trailed non sequiturs, his life catalyzed by impulse. He was not ready for the States, he said, he'd get there when he got there. He had to see, to see! He rose periodically from Jerry's mattress to his knees to stare outside at the humid mission lawns spreading from the sun-marbled hangar. Stretch marks like tribal scars radiated alongside his lower back.

She would follow him out the door to explore the dilapidated mission, the stained concrete hospital and the school empty for summer, as well as the hangar housing now only the slight Cessna trainer. Max rushed ahead with enthusiastic authority as if he were the tour guide, answering his own booming tenor questions with long-winded speculations.

By Wednesday morning his horizons had swelled; he wanted to leave the mission to experience the jungle.

"O.K.," said Jerry, "we'll visit the pygmies. Amosi will take us. He built my shed."

"Really?" Max pulled on his pants, cinching the belt so his waistband folded. His clothes bulged where he'd lost weight. "Seems like this area runs on pygmies. I used to think pygmies were elusive creatures you had to coax into contact, like black elves."

"They're not all so industrious. You'll see."

Amosi led them with dignified glee, head bobbing, Max barreling into him from behind each time Amosi halted to point his red cap at fleeing monkeys. Jerry hung behind, squinting her eyes out of focus so Max and Amosi were mere dabs against a screen of yearning ferns. The distant canopy dimmed the peat floor yet contained the heat so she felt like a bug caught in a kettle of steaming broccoli.

A path wound at times between walls of newly hacked brush and vines graced by weird orchids, but mostly it advanced freely beside the mammoth folds of giant trunks. An hour must have passed before they reached the clearing dotted with lumpy shelters: hollow humps of bound banana leaves standing shorter than Jerry. A similarly woven rectangular roof supported by four sticks covered a group of men sitting on stools. Elsewhere, women and children were scattered near fires, ambling and stirring. Everyone was naked except for loincloths open in the back like half-diapers. Four feet was the average height.

Amosi threw his cap, which began to fly hand to hand; Jerry accepted a triangular stool from an elder and waited for the circulating bamboo water pipe. Red-eyed, faces smeared with pleasure, the pygmies paid her little attention, speaking rarely even to each other. Meanwhile, Max photographed, a white giant galumphing hut to hut, shaking hands with women, stepping back then advancing, twisting behind his camera like a dancer behind a mask.

Amosi disappeared into his wife's hut and Jerry settled into the camp's watery rhythm, pulling at the pipe when she found it in her hands. She loved the pygmies, had dreamed of them tiny enough to fit in her palm, to climb lamps and swing from curtains, to scale the bamboo cross or surprise her in pockets. Here at their site she felt sadly apart, handicapped because she could not participate in their communal thoughts. Each visit she smoked and smoked, then stood unsteadily to hear the oceanic roars of their disappointment in her white weakness, and her feeling of distance would grow whiter and bigger as Amosi led her home, reeling, hopelessly civilized.

Max was crawling through a doorway, examining the banana leaf construction. Jerry turned to the old man beside her, who she knew spoke English, who had worked like Amosi among the Bantu but then retired back to his people.

"Do you have a totem?" she asked.

"Eh?"

She explained about the ancestral spirit. The elder inhaled, exhaled, as if the wet air were a drug, as if her idea, and she, too, were a drug. "We are the forest people," he said.

"The trees, then?"

"Eh."

"All of them? All the animals, too?"

Again he grunted assent. Of course, she thought, of course. His whole world a totem. Max pushed toward them, the hut shivering in his wake. Not wanting to trust his weight to a stool, he hunkered down, his exaggerated solemnity as he puffed once on the passing pipe reminding Jerry of a history book pioneer powwowing with Indians. Jerry laughed with everyone else, wishing she understood the source of their unanimous joy. Why didn't their drug make her see?

Max, soon bored with the grinning community, swerved to his feet — to Jerry everything not immobile was now swerving — and said that maybe they should go. Max shook hands with each man and she did the same, turning finally to see him shrunken at the clearing edge, waiting for her, from that distance pygmy size. She tramped after him, yelling, "You're a pygmy, an albino pygmy over there!"

When she reached him and he was realistically tall again, she tugged on his arm and breathed, "I love pygmies."

He pulled her forward so her feet felt like wheels turning themselves, circling, circling like his little chant. He was singing, amiably silly, and she trilled, complementing his rolling lines, "We're all albino pygmies on this bus!"

"No," she stopped suddenly, jerking him back. "No, tell me, who are you really?"

"Bogart. Humphrey Bogart in *The African Queen*."

She had not seen it, told him she'd grown up uncultured.

"A river captain. Scruffy."

"Huh," she said. "I'm Amelia Earhart."

Moving forward again, Max chanted, "Save the pygmies! Save the pygmies!" He grabbed a stick and waved it, a rioting demonstrator without a banner.

Jerry doubled over laughing. "You mean like their souls?"

"No, not their souls." He turned, huffing, ridiculously tortured. "Their bodies. Their souls are fine. It's their bodies we must save, as well as our own! We must save them from the ravages of civilization, we must save the world from nuclear war, we must save the whales, the manatees, everything!" The undulating stick smacked overhanging leaves.

"Manikins?"

"No, mana*tees*, those cow-dolphins in Florida and New Guinea! You don't know? You, we must save *your* soul!"

"Yes, save me, save me," she giggled, arms open wide.

Yet they froze amidst the approach of a terrible grinding echo from the west, then from straight above and all around as if they were embowelled in an angry lion, then receding to the east: her father's plane. She slowed, trying to think why this should make her uneasy, but when Max asked cheerfully if that was the pilot who could fly him to Fufalba, she realized yes, it was, that transportation had arrived for Max and that she would go, too, although she did not tell him then. Like a blow the mechanical thunder had struck her dumb, tangled her thoughts like vines so she had to concentrate just to figure out what she was thinking.

Finally they arrived to find Randolph trembling and contorted before the house, vibrating mysteriously so Jerry wondered what could make his cheeks deflate, his eyebrows stand like a frightened cat's fur, his finger reach jerking at her face: was this love? She felt herself soften but his fingers arced down toward her neck, she felt his split-second reptilian scrabbling at her cross, and pressure at the back of her neck pulling her forward as the chain snapped. He stood like a plaster saint holding out his fist, the two gold strands dangling. Then his fist approached; she waited stunned and solid as a martyr, yet what hit her cheek was not flesh but the cool metal tap of the cross. It fell sparkling to the grass.

Jerry had forgotten Max until her father lifted his gaze past her shoulder and shot his laser look; she imagined the smoky zap and fizz of disintegrating flesh and was not surprised when she turned to find empty lawn, Max gone.

Her father shrank toward the hangar, she was sure with dragon eyes aflame that might any second electrify the structure to blinding nothingness, might extinguish the mission, the full stretch of primeval forest, everything, so only he and she would float suspended in the black universe like stars light years apart.

In her bedroom she found atop the mussed sheets three pieces of the bamboo cross, one an angle like a boomerang, and the scattered contents of Max's shaving kit. He must have left it in the bathroom. She sensed freedom somehow mingled with disaster. She'd never felt so free. She picked up the right angle of the cross and walked outside. She threw hard, as hard as she could through the forest's rim, and waited for a thump. She waited a long time. Nothing came back.

No one ran from Jerry without a chase. Yet she waited all night in her shed, staring down the parrots, before taking off after Max. All night, drugged numb, a captive of her racing brain, she sat. Images alternated: her father stalled in the sky, horrified and helpless, permanently stuck in the moment before the dive; and Max urging her up a mountain trail, pointing out handholds, never too far ahead. Toward morning, however, she had to do something. While her father sulked in his hangar, clanging and thumping forebodingly, Jerry gathered her warmest clothes and some money from his desk.

Max was not at the roadside. She guessed that he'd caught a night truck and gone on, that the road was open. After a few hours' wait she flagged down her own transport truck to the highlands, and asked at stops along the way if a white man had been through. Fifty hours after bumping through jungle, dipping in and out of the crumbling road, waiting at the worst holes for makeshift repairs, she found Max in a village cafe.

"I can go myself," she said right away. "I don't have to climb with you."

Despair emanated from behind his coffee cup, that and the same original sweaty odor. "Why are you following me?" he sighed.

He did not want her. She saw that, now, looking from his dirty yellow hair to his crusty hand on the table, his jagged fingernails blindly poised alongside a puddle of spilled coffee. His smell was one of worthless cruelty, she decided, or perhaps just worthlessness. What had she wanted with him, anyway? Something had turned inside out; she cringed, knowing it was herself and not he who had changed, that he'd never wanted her.

Unable to accept that she'd come so far only to be rejected by a man she no longer wanted, she decided to go on. Max or no Max, she meant to climb a mountain, and in a flurry of self-sufficiency she stalked outside to pay her fare on the truck immediately leaving for the high country. Taking her seat in the vast cab, she was not the least surprised when Max appeared in the cafe doorway, wiping his mouth with the back of his hand. Passengers were climbing in the back, but he circled to the hood, dragging his pack, squinting dubiously at her from the windshield. Obviously, he'd been counting on riding comfortably in the cab, but not beside her, and only when the driver smacked him on the back and pointed, did Max swallow his pride and take his place at Jerry's elbow.

As the truck lurched into the road, Max shook his head. "Your father's strange."

"I know." She hesitated, surprised. Max had quit joking. It was as if a wall had been pushed over; they could see each other now. "So, what do you think about him? I mean, as an objective observer?"

He shrugged. "He's a religious fanatic."

"But why?"

Max scratched ineffectually at an insect smeared against the other side of the windshield. "He's making himself suffer for something he feels guilty about, I guess. Typical missionary. He doesn't like himself or anyone else."

"He must hate me."

"No. He's just protective."

Jerry studied Max's lumpy profile, her resentment tinged with new respect. He was right.

She had to go back. Yet she had to think of herself, for herself, to not lose this objectivity. Shouldn't she first climb the mountains? Max hadn't said get lost, but he wasn't encouraging, either.

"Where are you going, after these mountains?" she asked.

"Me? Asia. That's where the real mountains are, Nepal, you know, and all those people in nirvana."

"You're going to be a Buddhist." She liked that idea.

"Sure. Had enough of these missionaries out here."

Oriental philosophy had always intrigued Jerry. Ascetic introspection seemed a good approach to life. She could try that, she thought, yes she could. But not with Max.

They rolled along, faster and straighter as the road improved; they were nearing the edge of the trees, where the plateau would begin. Fufalba sat across the savannah at the foot of the snow-capped range. She fell asleep, woke up in the open plains. The truck was braking before a herd of huge birds.

Each creature was a hunched ball of dusty feathers on spindly legs, the eyes set meanly in a long yellow bill like a helmet. On the head and neck was dirty naked flesh fuzzed sparsely. A pink neck pouch flapped in the breeze like an empty breast.

As the truck passed, the storks hopped aside. Further ahead were more. Whole congregations lined the ditches. The driver told Jerry that they often blocked the road, scavenging for trash. Marabou, they were called. Chuckling, he said they ate water beetles, rats, termites, snakes, dead things, anything. Spying on prey from flight, they avoided the forest, nesting often in the baobabs of bush country. Max called the birds ugly vultures, but Jerry noted that when soaring they opened into beauty, black wings and white underbellies pinned to the sky.

Marabou were what she needed, she decided, not mountains. She would fill her shed. At Fufalba she descended alone from the truck, waving Max on, exhausted from the rancid cab, sick of her own stench as well as Max's, but satisfied. If she saw him again, it would be in the clouds, flying. From an airplane window, her shoulder pressed against the concave wall, she would scan the fluffy terrain and spot him perched like a guru on a tuft of cloud. He would not be bald, though, as monks are, but camouflaged—a white beard, a snow of hair. Her father had been sighting her mother wispily floating way up there for years, Jerry was sure.

Before Jerry turned around and hailed a truck back to Baku, she paid a man in Fufalba to find two marabou. She put them squawking, clacking beaks, in a large crate with the top nailed tight. She refused trucks for two days until one driver allowed the crate in the cab, away from the jostling cargo.

Arriving home, she found her father tinkering in his hangar, peeking at her from behind a detached propeller. She had to do something. She puttered in her shed, combatting decay; wood was not such a wise choice for building in the tropics. Already the floor in one corner was rotting, sinking down in the soft foundation.

Dinnertime she appeared at his table. He would not look up, barely ate. She was ravenous after her days in trucks, on the road, and heaped her plate twice with beans. He sat stiffly as she wiped her dish clean with a roll.

"Dad," she said. "Please come see my marabou."

His face lifted, the fine hair at his temples quivering, his caterpillar eyebrows pulling together above eyes turned away. He rose, and when she walked outside and down the path she heard his footsteps behind.

Twilight had already dimmed the interior and she lit the lamp. The marabou glowed, beaks curved like machetes, a perfect size for the large cages. Amosi had taken away the bitter parrots; the marabou would not tolerate them, but beat their huge wings so hard against the wire cage that Jerry had been afraid they would break.

The shed was tidy. Shadows from the lamp danced across the empty table, from which she had removed the aeronautics books. Buddhism was what she would study now; she would find material in Bashushi, teach herself Sanskrit.

Her father was waiting outside. Was he afraid of the dark?

"Come on in, they're inside here."

Wary, he stepped up and shuffled across the floorboards, eyes adjusting to the oceanic green light. Unaccustomed to the murkiness, he put up his arms awkwardly, pumping slightly as if to keep from drowning and stood as if ready to run, disoriented, out of his mechanical element. He did not see the birds. His eyes settled finally on Jerry's and instead of laser beams she saw age, the sudden tentative wrinkles flickering in the lamp's gleam. His eyes pale and faltering were what she saw, his eyes wrapped in an embroidery of lichen.

A Walk
Down
the Beach

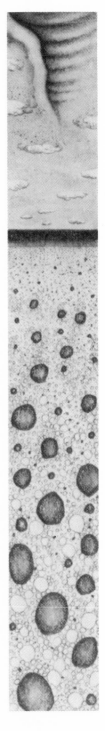

Within limits, Alice could ignore the house arrest. Martin was at work, over at the Embassy. The American school had closed for the moment, though, and Renee at home had made these days more like summer. To Alice it felt like any tropical morning as she watched Sunny, the houseboy, wipe the kitchen counters.

She could hear Renee splashing in the pool. After the *waflop* of her dolphin dive, the arc from chest-high in the shallow end, Renee would stay submerged as long as possible, being a mermaid. For minutes Alice would hear nothing as Renee came up stealthily for air, hugging the pool first at one side, then another, slipping down and up again, until she found it safe enough to repeat the dolphin splash. Alice had often watched the game from a poolside table as she wrote letters home or struggled with French grammar or simply read one of the dog-eared spy novels that circulated among the American community. Looking up, she would see Renee, a fast blur underwater. She'd see also, beyond the pool, beyond the fence, the stretch of lumpy volcanic rocks dotted with native kids fishing or crustacean hunting. The Atlantic was a horizontal ribbon. And across all that ocean, so blue and cool, was home, Maryland.

These past few days, waiting and waiting, Alice had found herself pushing aside the French subjunctive for a better distraction: Renee's books. Magic nannies and talking lions; secret worlds with their own rules. The week's suspense had changed other things, too. Renee now had permission to swim alone. She had to have some freedom, stuck home without friends, without even her puppy. Although what happened to Dusty had nothing to do with this house arrest.

On the kitchen counters Alice drew circles with white chalk around the jars of flour, sugar, corn flakes, and cookies. Renee's hobby of making cookies had flourished, and the ants had multiplied. Normally Alice kept Renee's baking in check, fearing cavities as well as her own thickening waist and thighs; even in Africa the inspiring image of Jackie Kennedy, so trim and jaunty in her pillbox, worked in Alice as an alarm against calories. But things were not normal and keeping busy was best, so Renee baked.

"*Comme ça*," Alice said, turning to Sunny. Like this. His skin was very black and his hair mottled with grey, but the name "Sunny" fit his bright inquisitiveness. Alice assumed that some early Foreign Service wife had nicknamed Sunny when his real Guinéan name was too hard to pronounce. She had decided to think of him as "Sunny" and not "Sonny," since he was anything but childlike. The houseboy uniform of starched white shorts and shirt, so cute on a boy, was absurd on this old man. She should get long trousers tailored for him, she saw that now, peering into his eyes. The eyes worried her. Yellow and watery, they appeared jaundiced. What if Renee were being exposed to hepatitis? He might have to go. The gamma globulin shots didn't always work. Alice gauged how long until the half-year boosters were due; their first injections had been back in Washington, a month before leaving. November now. They'd only been here four months?

No, she decided, tracing a circle around the flour jar, she couldn't sack Sunny just because his eyes were yellow. All the natives' were. He was clean and good. He played so well with Renee, clasping her by the forearms and swinging her around and around in the garden. Renee called it flying. *"Voler, voler vite,"* she would nag Sunny. Once, as Alice watched Renee revolve around the flash of Sunny's grin, her brown pageboy a tornado, her tan legs stiff as a rudder, something surged. Alice's eyes burned and blotted as she joined the laughter, and it seemed the leaves and branches, the green itself, was laughing. The sudden teariness confused her: was she happy or sad? Or just very alive? She had never felt so full, never while watching Martin with Renee. Alice had never seen such a grip, double arm clasps, between her husband and daughter. What here was missing in their frequent hugs?

Alice blinked at Sunny, who gazed seriously at her chalk circles. She calculated her next phrase, resenting French. She should be fluent by now, after those deadly State Department classes Martin had sent her to after he'd got his assignment. For this first overseas post they'd actually given her homework, back in Washington. As if she, as well as Martin, were an employee obligated to measure up.

Ants, she remembered, *fourmi.*

"Comme ça, Sunny. The ants don't like chalk. They won't come, won't enter." Hopping her finger across one white line, she pressed a manicured nail to the tiled counter. Then, *"Pas,"* waving the hand, no. If her French was not improving, her sign language, at least, was.

"Oui, oui, Madame," he nodded encouragingly, eyebrows raised. *"Oui."*

Accepting the chalk, he drew his own circle outside of hers, following her curve. His knuckles bulged; he'd developed callouses like gloves. Alice had seen him pull casseroles from the oven barehanded and not flinch.

"Yes, good. Now we do this each place the ants go. We don't like ants."

"No ants," Sunny said.

Gravel crunched in the drive: a car. What now? Midmorning, too early for Martin's lunch—but what was she thinking? He hadn't been home for lunch since this started. She watched

Sunny run to the kitchen door, lean out, and swivel back with the information, "It's the doctor."

Awfully early for William. Would the guard block the gate, feet apart, rifle held out parallel to his body like a barrier? He took this stance each time a car passed; Alice had watched from the bedroom window. She hadn't yet seen the rifle pointed.

William this early for his daily visit meant perhaps that something was happening downtown. So far, Alice's routine had not varied, not from the moment she woke to hear the military truck's groan as the night soldier's replacement arrived. Martin would be at the window peeking through the curtain, his hunched shoulders angry and helpless in his blue pajamas.

That morning she had seen his bent figure as innards missing a shell, an interior she didn't know. The real Martin leaned back on his heels, told good stories, and rubbed his hands together as if everything had just been resolved. He had always been a ladies' man. Dark and sleek, aristocratically fine-boned and mannered, he pulled out chairs, looked you in the eye slightly too long, singled you out. When they'd met, Alice had played hard to get, amused by his hand on her back as they navigated the university crowds. Now, as an initiate of the overseas life of cocktail parties, she understood how Martin's personality worked. He was a diplomat.

Hiding at the window, he was something less. His identity existed outside of his pajamas, outside of the house, over near the black guards in green uniforms and the truck pulling away. It existed in the strident tones of Africanized French broadcast in the streets by the government's propaganda bus: "*Pas d'impérialisme! Pas d'Américains!*" And, during the hour he showered, dressed, and drank his coffee, Martin kept himself wired to that outside identity through the radio, alternating VOA with BBC with the local Conakry station.

"Keep tuning in," he had said as he kissed her, missing her mouth, reaching behind her for his briefcase. But he stopped and held her, and they rocked slightly to a Beatles song on BBC. "*Michelle, ma belle,*" he sang, and said, "Things are calming down."

Alice swayed with him, her nose at his shoulder. She sang, too: "*vont très bien ensemble. Très bien ensemble.*" She was glad the Beatles had a French song—for her, almost. Sung, the language was beautiful, so much better than her spoken over-enunciation. Then the familiar irritation pricked and she stepped away, apart. Martin looked puzzled, his low forehead creasing, and Alice felt sorry, wanting to like him, until he smiled the charming smile that went with his dark suit.

From the door, he called, "Just wait 'til we get back with our Tarzan stories, Alice. And Renee, what an education!"

Alice imagined Renee in Maryland where no men with guns closed schools. She switched back to VOA, hoping for American music, but someone was talking about Johnson and civil rights. She turned the radio off, not even trying Radio Guinea. The French was too hard, and she didn't want to know what was happening anyway because what could she do? To Alice an amorphous riot was not half the threat of the rifle outside her gate. She didn't want to know.

Now, dropping the chalk into a drawer, she heard raised voices: William trying to talk his way past the guard. Where was Renee? He shouldn't have arrived until three or so. Only he, as Embassy doctor, was allowed to visit the house; he was her link to outside, he centered her routine. Morning housework, lunch with Renee, poolside reading, William and the rabies shots, calisthenics in the water, then Martin.

Making Renee's Halloween costume had kept her busy, too, as had fixing the treats for the school Halloween party, which hadn't been held last night. At the dinner table, Renee had studied her spaghetti, so all Alice could see of her disappointment was the long curly eyelashes.

Beside Sunny at the kitchen door, she watched William get out of his aqua Valiant parked shaded by the acacia. For a second their eyes met, by accident on his part; he looked away. He wanted to arrive calm and avuncular, she guessed, but she had glimpsed him before the act. Eyes tightened, mouth pursed, exhaling—had he been breathing deeply, as he advised her?

William briskly slammed the car door and crunched toward her with the authority of his black medicine case. "I'm early, but I was out at Sloans'. One of the kids has the flu." His expression now was composed and direct, eyes steady behind his black-rimmed glasses, his stride controlled so that his large frame reassured rather than threatened. Large men usually made Alice uneasy.

His real performance, however, did not begin until he'd settled inside, bag open on the dining table, arms washed, as if he needed props and ritual to remind him of his role. As the friendly country doctor he could convince Alice to talk about herself as she might to either a close friend or a total stranger she'd never see again. She resented this power of William's not because she told him any real secrets—she didn't—but because she knew nothing of him.

He told her nothing of what was happening, either. She would ask about downtown: were people marching, had buildings been damaged? He wouldn't know, every day. Martin trusted her with details, but maybe some husbands wouldn't and William was afraid of interfering. Through Martin's fast words and pantomime all aspects of Touré's antics accrued nightly in the bedroom. The worst scenario Alice was glad she hadn't seen: three cabinet ministers, Touré's critics, hung from a highway overpass. Martin drove underneath, gagging, he'd said. Alice pictured shoes skewed, floating up the windshield.

She witnessed Martin's dramas as he paced and stood. His facade was wrong in their bedroom, as strange as the vulnerable window figure in pajamas—and that was the new, soft Martin she needed to understand but couldn't reach; he stiffened with plastic reassurance each time she came near.

As William fished inside his case Alice resisted her own curiosity, standing nonchalantly aside instead of asking why he was *really* there early. If he was watching to gauge her stability, she was not going to appear worried.

"Ahah," he said, smiling at her waist, "You've been chalking your kitchen, I see. Barbara likes that, too. She says it works, and I never see any ants."

Alice brushed at herself where she had absentmindedly wiped the white dust. "Barbara's the one who told me. At the Franklins'."

She felt her cheeks flush as she remembered ranting and raving about the ants, the termites, the cockroaches. She'd been a little in shock at that party, over two weeks ago, after William's first house visit. That morning he had arrived to begin the rabies vaccines as well as to shoot poor Dusty, whose crazy barks had echoed in the locked garage like screeching tires—up until the crash of the gun.

Barbara had taken charge of Alice, plying her with drink after drink in the obscure patio corner, suggesting remedies. "White chalk. It's got to be white, don't ask me why. Something about it repels ants, you'll see them massing at the line like it's a wall. Darlene in the school office gives it away. Ask Renee to bring some home."

Unlike her husband William, Barbara talked so much that she quickly relieved Alice's urge to babble. Alice nodded toward the clumps of other guests and the paper lanterns strung to palm tree trunks. Barbara had her own role, not so much the Doctor's Wife as the Veteran Expatriate, practical from her short shapeless hairstyle to her biting sense of humor. Everything was worth at least a laugh.

Alice recalled the throaty smoker's laugh as William drew serum from a vial into the hypodermic needle. She saw again Dusty's gold fur and the long-haired tail and the sudden snarl and snap that had met her own hand reaching to check the crusted gash behind Dusty's silky ear. She remembered coaxing Dusty into the garage and locking the door just in case he had been bitten by a rabid dog, sure she was over-reacting. But she hadn't been. Renee had buried Dusty's dishes, brush, tennis ball and towel instead of Dusty because William had taken the carcass to send a brain sample to the Munich lab.

He seemed to follow her train of thought. "How's Renee enjoying her vacation?" He looked blankly around, as if he might have missed her in the room.

Alice smiled. She and Martin and William, too, now, referred to this house arrest as Renee's vacation since the American school had been suspended.

"She missed the Halloween party. She was really looking forward to it, you know, with the costume and treats and everything. I think she's almost starting to miss school. There's no one for her to play with here."

"She wore her costume, anyway, didn't she? Brad and Jim did, they were running circles around the house, trying to scare Kofi." The empty vial set aside, William held the needle daintily up, and grabbed some disinfectant cotton with his other hand. "I'll go on and do Sunny, then you, and then we can look for Renee. Is she off reading again?"

"Swimming. She wouldn't wear her costume. She's at that age where her parents aren't so fun to play with any more. If she'd had someone to dress up for, if you'd been here, she might have. Sometimes I wish she had brothers and sisters."

"Be right back." He went toward the kitchen, where Sunny would be waiting. William had recommended that everyone who normally petted Dusty have the series of twenty-one injections. That included everyone in the house but Martin.

Alice went to the patio and scanned the yard. The bougainvillea needed pruning; the magenta branches poked and dangled across the path so only fragments of pool water were visible. From the wet trail on the stones, however, Alice knew Renee had already come up.

At Renee's bedroom door, Alice knocked. "The doctor's here, Renee, he's almost ready for you." Because it seemed important to respect her daughter's privacy, Alice had made rules: always knock, never lock doors. Renee should never feel the need to lock doors.

"Don't come in," came Renee's muffled voice.

Was she so modest already, only nine? "All right, but hurry now," Alice called.

Back in the dining room, William was pulling serum into another syringe. He turned around so Alice couldn't watch her own treatment prepared.

"About what you said, about those brothers and sisters, it's not too late, you know. You're still young."

"No," said Alice. "No. I'd only want them for Renee, not for me, and she's too old to play with babies." She wondered why the idea was so distasteful. She had expected other kids after Renee but none had come, and now she was on the pill. William, of course, knew this. But not the moment of her decision, a few years ago, that Martin and she should stop trying. He had agreed that they were beyond babies, that Renee was enough. Alice winced at the cold fact that babies came from something they no longer shared.

For Alice's shot she stepped into her and Martin's bedroom. The air conditioner was off, the air still, slightly moldy. Having another man in their room, even William, confused Alice, especially when she pulled up her dress and pulled back her underwear. Today, however, was a left arm day. Thank God they no longer gave them in the stomach; that would hurt worst.

What William did was to rotate the injections. She'd actually got in the habit of calculating, as she dressed in the morning, where her shot would be that day—left or right arm, left or right hip—so that she saved her decent cotton briefs for William. The frayed ones and the red and black satin ones she saved for the arm days when he wouldn't see. After she'd set aside her cotton pairs, the satin ones had surfaced from the bottom of her drawer; she'd forgotten about them, an anniversary gift from Martin.

"Relax," said William, "relax. Think of Switzerland, those snowy peaks, the wine." So long away. She didn't believe this post would last until next summer for that R&R, but for the sake of the injection she imagined the craggy peaks, Renee in Lederhosen.

After the first couple of days, the shots had lost their sting, and Alice realized how much of pain was fear. She pictured Swiss cottages like dollhouses as William gripped her arm, as it ached in a rush. She was not afraid, and it was over.

"Have you been using the Thorazine?" William insisted on their moment of privacy, even when she didn't have to pull up her dress, so that he could ask these questions. A daily consultation.

"Yes," she lied. Then, afraid he could tell she wasn't, "Just at night." When he'd left her a bottle the first day of house arrest she'd been insulted. Damned if she were going to sit through this like a zombie. Drugging wives when things got tense was apparently normal procedure in the Foreign Service. After all, what could multilingual hostesses do when deprived of their bridge parties? "Barbara finds the pills helpful," William had said. When Alice told Martin he had joked, missing the point. "Well, don't throw them out. If you don't need them, I might."

William looked up from his empty syringe. She felt him assessing her, checking for problems. Wasn't she acting normally, handling the incident well? She was calm. She rubbed the arm, and shook her bangs out of her eyes.

So William would know that she had things in perspective, she said, "Touré's going to run out of steam."

William nodded. "Or if he doesn't, the rest of Africa will. He can hate imperialism, but he can't hate black Africa. He's supposed to be defending Africa, but the OAU is already coming down on him. He's an irrational fool."

Alice swung her arm to keep her muscles from knotting later, feeling victory. William had condescended to talk politics! So she was passing his test. Before moving to the door, she asked, "So why are you *really* here early?"

William looked down at her, too tall up close. He seemed to share her unease, and stepped backward. "People are near the *Corniche*, now, headed for the Ambassador's house. We want all the families in one place, as much as possible. You and Renee can walk down the beach to Breusmans'; it's about three miles. Go about one, the tide's low then. Don't go after two, the tide will be starting back in. It's rocky for about two miles, then you get beach." He was watching.

She nodded, going over questions silently, answering them all herself. The "people" were citizens incited by Touré's broadcast denunciations of Americans. What about the armed guard whose purpose was supposedly to protect the house from ri-

144   BLUE TAXIS

oters? Clearly, the soldiers were meant to intimidate the Americans more than the rioters. Alice immediately liked the idea of escape.

"I won't say anything to Renee for a while," she said. "She spies on the guard, maybe even talks to him. I've told her not to, but she's so bored. She might make him suspicious without knowing what she's doing."

They looked at each other a minute.

"Around one?"

"Right. There's a two-way radio at the Breusmans' to contact the Embassy, and all the oceanfront families will be there. Don't pack anything, just look like you're walking down the beach. Try to look European, not American. Whatever that means." He squeezed a smile.

Alice led the way to the dining room, and as they came out of the hall something burst shrieking from under the table. Alice gasped, both hands at her mouth, then yelled. "Renee!"

But Renee was doubled over laughing, the cardboard tail angling out unnaturally from where Alice had sewn it onto Renee's sweat pants. William was laughing too. Although Alice resented being tricked she had to admit the elephant costume was good. Renee straightened and wagged her trunk, made from Alice's hose stuffed with shreds of old curtains dyed grey. The trunk hung from a hood made of the same fabric, with great flopping ears.

"I scared *you!*" Renee shouted.

"My God, what is this creature?" William said, heading for his black bag, Alice guessed, to prepare Renee's shot while her spirits were still high.

"A unique wild specimen," he went on. "I must sedate it so we can study it back at the animal station." He tilted another needled vial in the air.

He was good with children, better than with wives, Alice decided. His injection method with Renee was less abstract than imaginary Alps.

"Can this creature count, I wonder? Is this an intelligent species?"

Renee's task was to count from fifteen backwards, to race to finish before the needle did. She never won. Bunching up her sleeve at the shoulder, she turned away her elephant head and began to count, punctuating her numbers with elephant neighs.

"Alrighty," William said, finished. "Now where's that little girl who collects syringes?"

Renee eagerly took off her elephant mask. Nearly fifty syringes must have accumulated in her shoe box by now. After whatever vaccination booster—not just the rabies shots needed by a number of people exposed to rabies—William offered the syringes, needles removed, to children. The kids used them in water fights around the pool; Alice had watched them stalking and squirting water down backs and in ears, falling play-dead when ammo ran short. Once she'd seen native children at the fence, their hands and noses pushing against the wire as they tried to understand the plastic toy water game. Usually Alice shooed them away, but this time she had found herself stuck, seeing through their eyes. According to Barbara the Guinéans believed white people's medicine to be poison, that injections were meant to weaken and kill so whites could steal land.

Renee ran after William, her awkward tail pumping, as he went to the kitchen to wash the syringes. Alice was slightly surprised but glad that Renee did not hate him for shooting Dusty. Some resentment would have been normal, yet Renee had maturely accepted the fact that William had cut short Dusty's pain.

As Alice reached the kitchen, Renee was dragging the cookie jar across its chalk circle so she could reach to open the lid.

"Don't worry, Mom, this is for Doctor William, not me." Renee held out to William a ginger snap from yesterday's batch, and he traded his syringes.

"I bet you've got more of these than both my sons, now. You're going to be a real terror."

Licking crumbs from her fingers, Renee said, "I can win anyway, even with less. It's not how many you have, but strategy."

Strategy. Such a boy word. But better that Renee be tough

than damaged, Alice told herself, wondering then whether they weren't the same thing.

William was waving his half-eaten cookie at her from the door. "Beautiful day for a walk."

Suddenly her fingertips burned, her temples wanted to explode, and the walls yawned. "Wait."

Just as quickly she felt all right. William munching in the doorway looked reassuringly calm as his eyes questioned her: something wrong?

"Nothing," she said, turning to the smudged chalk. One ant crawled back and forth outside the border, missing the way in.

Alice stood beside the pool, looking for Renee. Not yet noon, early for lunch; but they had to eat and get ready for the walk. The weather was perfect. While the ocean breeze tempered the heat, the bright November sun glazed everything. The rocks were purple, the distant water solid, and the mammoth cactus at Alice's elbow an eerie chartreuse. Who would plant cactus near a pool? Someone without children, without the automatic image of a child falling into thorns.

So alive and accessible, the landscape still hid certain things. The islands to the west were invisible, curtained by an impenetrable haze. Alice had seen them a few times after storms. She remembered a couple of months ago, August it must have been, before the monsoons ended and Renee's school began, a huge thunderstorm combined with a high tide had thrown fish into the pool. Alice squinted at the ocean—about half a mile away now, where it belonged. What had that water been doing here, splashing waves into her chlorinated pool?

Hard to believe how, after the night of roaring gusts that had made the house bang and shudder, she had got up to find Sunny so excited. *"Poissons dans la piscine,"* he kept saying as he set the table. Fish in the pool. Renee ran outside without tying her shoelaces. By the time Alice had got Sunny started on Martin's eggs, Renee had taken charge of the fish. Alice found her with a bucket of sea water already fetched from tidepools, dipping the long-handled skimming net through the pool. Four fish were dead, on their sides on the concrete, but two wriggled weakly in the bucket.

"There's still two more," Renee shouted, puffing. "If I can get them in salt water they might live."

Idiotically, Alice had expected a utopian aquarium with fish spurting and darting above the sparkling tile floor. She marvelled at Renee's presence of mind. Only nine.

Renee had run around to the deep end; leaning over the water, she strained to poke the net deep. "They all go in the middle," she said. Her small face was pink, bunched like a fist. When she turned her head suddenly, her hair swiveled and rose like a top. Little legs splayed, arms way out over the edge, she was perfectly balanced, would not fall in.

"Want me to try?" Not really wanting to, Alice stepped around. Either she'd fall or fail to catch the fish. Something would go wrong. Why did she always feel this way about herself lately? Where was her agility? She had gained only five pounds since college, but she felt so much heavier, slower, more stupid. Since moving here she often felt younger than Renee.

But she accepted the net from Renee, feeling it drag.

"It's over to the right, see it? Sitting there, not even moving. It's easy, I just can't reach it." Renee's brown eyes glistened, her bangs splintered above the eyebrows.

Leaning slightly, not too much, Alice told herself she could. If she fell, so what? Renee would be disappointed. Alice would splash embarassingly, probably sink. Why this lack of confidence, though? — she'd always been a good swimmer. The net neared the dark knot in the water, pulled right past, and lifted with no resistance. The fish was there.

"You got it, you got it," Renee yelled, already running for her bucket. "There's another one right by where that one was," she shouted toward the garden.

The second fish was equally easy. Then Renee had to hurry the four survivors to the ocean because the bucket was too cramped. And after that she was going to rescue all the fish caught in tidepools. Alice watched her open and close the gate, and hop her way across the rocks until she was a tiny dab. The idea of her daughter outside the gate worried her, but the idea of boxing Renee up was worse.

There had been a time Alice had felt older. When Martin and she had first married, when Renee was in diapers, Martin in graduate school, Martin in his first Washington assignments, right up until Guinea she had felt old enough. But here, unable to speak the language, she felt infantile — wary and helpless and inferior to her own daughter.

Steps had sounded on the walkway, Martin's quick steps.

"Look at those islands!" He was beside her, all soap and starched shirt, his arm raised pointing at the horizon.

So involved in the pool, the fish, her daughter, herself, Alice had not noticed them. "Oh, look," she agreed. They were violet and sturdy, a distant mountain range risen above the water at Martin's command.

Then his hand lay at her neck, fingering her collarbone.

"Scared last night?" he asked.

During the pummeling rain and the lightning almost frequent enough to replace the shorted electricity, with Renee between them in the bed, Alice had not admitted fear. "Yes," she said.

"Me, too. But this morning it all seems worthwhile. What a day — and fish in the pool! I see Renee's on top of things. She's lucky, she's got a child's paradise here."

Renee's dot was growing, an insect zigzagging, hopping rock to rock. For a second she disappeared, and Alice's heart lurched. Was Renee hurt? Martin was smiling blandly at the mountains. Alice had bit her lip, kept biting down until long after Renee was again visible.

And now, especially now, three months later in the stunning November noon, that fear would not stop. Where was Renee this moment, almost time for lunch? Out on the rocks a pale figure wavered. She knew to come in for lunch, and she would. A mother could not afford to worry before a child was late, that was all.

Renee was ready with a bulging straw sack of "things to do" which Alice had trusted her to pack, insisting only on the toothbrush. In her own woven basket Alice carried a supply of the Halloween treats. Earlier in the week they had prepared fifty baggies, each filled with M&M's and chocolate kisses from the commissary, peanuts that Sunny had shelled and roasted, and homemade coconut bars. The Breusman gathering would be a good chance to get rid of some.

Alice had often packed the African basket for picnics, although the best beach where everyone went Sundays was quite a drive. She had never taken a walk down her own shoreline, nor had she ever seen any other white person strolling past. Nevertheless, she might have, and today's walk might be simply recreational. It would have to look that way.

To look European was not easy for Alice. She'd always been happy with American clothes. Her fullskirted shirtwaist with the delicate iris print was her solution. She didn't have any of those straight-cut minis that were in the French magazines, that everyone was having tailored out of African print — such sleek space-age lines disturbed Alice. Shoes were the worst problem. The French women wore thick-soled, thick-strapped sandals good for rough walking, but she had only dainty heels, flip flops and tennis shoes. From below her billowing skirt the white sneaker toes taunted; only an American could dress so awkwardly.

Still tasting tuna fish from lunch, Alice led Renee out the pool gate.

"How far is it?" Renee wanted to know.

"A nice long walk. Three miles, maybe." Was her voice shaking? Brightly, she started the game. "How many kilometers?"

Renee had a good head for numbers and liked the challenge of Guinea's metric system. "My walking slide rule," Alice had called her, until one day Renee objected, "No! Slide rules don't do that, Daddy showed me. Slide rules don't tell those conversions."

Already several rocks ahead, Renee called back, "Five kilometers!"

Too far behind to continue the quiz, Alice watched Renee stop and flap her arms. Yellow shorts today. Renee had the same pair in five different, equally faded colors, and then the same assortment one size larger for when she grew and they could not find new Western clothes. The reserve assortment, still in boxes, was much darker. Every so often Renee would beg to try them on and Alice would pull them out, amused by how badly Renee wanted to grow. Ten years ago Martin had called Alice his knock-out, and he still bought her silk underwear, but she felt her shape going out of style. Models and actresses were skinnier, mirroring that lean Jackie, so pinched since Kennedy's death. The feminine ideal was shrinking.

Renee had skipped off to the side and was reaching down. As Alice drew parallel, balancing carefully on each jagged edge of rock, she shouted, "What'd you find?"

"Shells!"

Renee ran back to show her handful of tiny conch and snail shells, dappled trinkets.

"Lovely. Will you make me some earrings?"

This Renee took seriously, pursing her eyebrows and mouth, wondering how. "Fishing line," she answered her unspoken question. "I'll loop them through fishing line."

The distance accumulated in stretches. They would approach a natural jetty of rocks, climb above and around it, and head toward another point. The air smelled of salt, fish, and, in spots, feces. Alice hadn't known Africans defecated out here. More than the threat of Renee swept away by a surprise wave, or fallen from a rock, the idea of Renee stumbling through diseased feces alarmed Alice.

Around the next bend, Alice stopped and stared, the basket swinging. Not that elephant head again! It was emerging above a massive conglomeration of rock, like a fly crawling around dung. How had it got there? When would this stop? Alice felt tiny, engulfed in some disgusting refuse: a gnat.

Hysterical with giggles, Renee was jerking toward the rock. The elephant head rose up over the ten-foot high cliff, and spindly black arms appeared, waving. From behind came a chorus of

"Eeeeooo"—children playing elephant. The tiny body below the mask wore only ragged shorts: a boy.

What annoyed Alice was that she and Renee had spent days making the mask, and here breathing into it was a dirty native, probably ill. Already the trunk was splattered with mud.

"Renee!" she shouted, bending slightly at the knees, determined not to move until this was cleared up.

Renee turned from the chorus of laughter, her face brittle at the sound of Alice's voice. Then Renee's French lilted out and the children, four or five of them on the rock, quieted, drawing together. What had Renee said? How could her French be so good when Alice had been the one studying? There was a whole world out here that Renee loved, not make-believe like the mermaid place, but something real Alice could not understand. She felt like a child in one of Renee's books who realizes that magic is real, that if you open the right door lions can talk. And Renee spoke the language.

Eyes watering, wanting not to be bad, Renee trotted up to Alice's spot of sand between boulders. "I gave it to them. They liked it so much. I wore it earlier out to the pool and they saw through the fence, and I remembered how it scared you, so I gave it to them. For keeps. I can't be an Indian giver."

Alice softened. "It's all right, you meant well. Just understand that we can't stop to play. We're not supposed to be out here, we can't attract attention. And don't tell *them* that. Just say we have to hurry. You'll play tomorrow."

Alice moved forward, her feet rolling in the loose sand. Which rock would be easiest to climb? They were getting bigger here. She had backed off in the face of logic: what *was* she so upset about? Why should Renee's Guinéan friends be so frightening?

Sticking close, Renee turned around to watch Alice pick her way step by step. Alice saw the children squatting above as she passed. Like monkeys. Like monkeys at the fence when they stared in at the pool. But like humans, too, shut off from an oasis in their own land.

At the tip of the point, at their last view of the kids, Alice said, "Come on, let's wave good-bye." When they did the Guinéans, still watching, stood and rocked their hands back and forth. Voices carried: the communal elephant screech.

"How long have you known them?"

"I don't know them, really." Renee sounded defensive. "They just come to the fence a lot, and I talk to them, and when I go out there we play sometimes."

"What do you play?"

"We look for mussels, they eat them."

"Do you, too?"

Renee laughed. The way was getting sandier now, the rocks less encompassing. Alice congratulated herself on achieving this momentary intimacy with Renee. Recently motherhood felt best when they acted like equals.

"I ate one," Renee answered. "It was gross, like sand and salt. But I help find them."

"And what else?"

"We chase crabs. And they shoot at birds with slingshots."

Another crop of rocks began as they neared another jetty. "I thought you didn't like for animals to die. All those fish you saved."

"I know, but the Guinéans eat this stuff. It's not like just killing for fun. And I never shot at any birds."

Silently, they navigated the last point to see the shore open out into real beach. The rest would be easy, although they would be more visible. The unease lurked. Some mob would come in a dark, solid wave from inland, pouring over the coast road. Or an armed *gendarme* would rush from the trees, pointing a rifle.

Alice asked, "Are your friends nice?"

"I'll show you." Renee dug into her sack. "That boy with the mask, he gave me this. He gave me this first, that's why I gave him the mask. He didn't ask or anything."

She pulled out a large conch shell, something rare here in Guinea. Alice had seen them that size only in Maryland. The outside was calloused, like cement dried unevenly, but inside the creamy pinks and purples curled mysteriously inward. Holding the shell to her ear, Alice listened to the hollow roar and then to the real waves crashing.

"Do you hear the ocean?" Alice handed the shell to Renee, who shook it, then listened.

"That's an echo," she answered.

Inside the conch, then, was merely the memory of water and pulse, a ghost. At Renee's age, Alice had believed in the hidden ocean; her daughter's practicality was amazing. Yet she was sure that, even grown up, she heard some magic in the shell. Now she recognized the ocean rhythm as something she had come to take for granted. All around, she heard it everywhere, and nowhere; it was wrapped around her consciousness.

As they followed the water line on the sand, Alice wondered what went on in Renee's busy mind. Renee's brain seemed to have doors opening in odd places.

Alice's brain felt like Dusty's, isolated in a box. That sweet mind had been extracted from the wonderful fur and bright eyes. They'd got him from an English couple here, from their cocker spaniel's litter. Martin had wanted a guard dog, but Renee had wanted Dusty. So had Alice. How would you send a brain sample to Munich? A metal box, perhaps, packed in ice. The tissue could tick crazily away, harmless without its body, yet full of details. A detached universe.

They had reached the last stretch of beach before the Breusmans', and Renee's shoes dangled from her hand, her legs wet below the knees. Suddenly she rushed ahead toward a beige-skinned figure; one of her American friends. The Breusmans' house waited just there, the end of three miles. But Alice did not feel like she had arrived. She had only skirted Africa, that was all she could do. Martin had left her behind and gone in deep.

Yet she felt safe for the first time in months. She and Renee were going home to Maryland. Martin would stay, she knew. He might stay off forever; she might start on her own back at work, at school, because he would never give up his embassies and boondock countries. She tried to feel sad, but instead felt alive. It seemed she'd stopped missing him long ago. Would he mind her gone, would he even notice?

At the airport, three days later, she said good-bye. Touré had calmed down and lifted house arrest; the American school had re-opened. Martin was staying; Alice had been right about that. He said he understood. She wasn't sure he did, or that she did; things could change back in the States. Maybe he'd come home.

From the plane she saw him on the airport observation deck, his hands clasped as if while rubbing together they'd frozen. All of him so small, so pale. Alice wanted to unbuckle her seatbelt and run back. But the plane was swivelling, nosing toward the runway. Between Alice and the window sat Renee, eyes scrunched shut as Martin slid away, the huge conch pressed to her ear.

Eileen Drew was born in Casablanca, Morocco in 1957 and then moved every few years according to her father's assignments in the U.S. Foreign Service. She has lived in Lagos, Nigeria; Conakry, Guinea; Accra, Ghana; and was trained for the Peace Corps in Bukavu, Zaire. Drew spent the years of 1979–1981 as Instructor and School Librarian in Nsona Mpangu, Zaire. Currently, she teaches English as a Second Language at Mount Diablo Adult School in Concord, California. Through June 1988, she was Director of English as a Second Language for the Lao Family Community, Inc. in Richmond, California.

Her previous honors include: the Katherine Anne Porter Prize from *Nimrod*; the *Black Warrior Review* Literary Award; the Charles Angoff Award from *The Literary Review*; and, being named a finalist for the Drue Heinz Literature Prize. Ms. Drew received a Master of Fine Arts in Creative Writing from the University of Arizona, Tucson, in 1986, and a Bachelor of Arts from the University of California in Santa Cruz.